DESTRUCTION OF DISBELIEF

KENNIS ANTHONY

Order this book online at www.trafford.com
or email orders@trafford.com

Most Trafford titles are also available at major online book retailers.

Scripture quotations marked KJV are from the Holy Bible, King
James Version. First published in 1611. Quoted from the KJV Classic
Reference Bible (© 1983 by the Zondervan Corporation).

Cover Design by Lana Campbell

Print information available on the last page.

ISBN: 978-1-4907-5680-6 (sc)
ISBN: 978-1-4907-5682-0 (hc)
ISBN: 978-1-4907-5681-3 (e)

Library of Congress Control Number: 2015904283

Because of the dynamic nature of the Internet, any web addresses or links contained in
this book may have changed since publication and may no longer be valid. The views
expressed in this work are solely those of the author and do not necessarily reflect the
views of the publisher, and the publisher hereby disclaims any responsibility for them.

Any people depicted in stock imagery provided by Thinkstock are models,
and such images are being used for illustrative purposes only.
Certain stock imagery © Thinkstock.

Trafford rev. 03/23/2015

Trafford
PUBLISHING® www.trafford.com
North America & international
toll-free: 1 888 232 4444 (USA & Canada)
fax: 812 355 4082

Contents

1. MOVE FAST, YOU MUST

While nervously holding his right hand inches over the abort button and clinching a satellite phone with his left hand, Eric Miller advises Elizabeth Devereaux from his lab somewhere in the Ceres Asteroid Belt to pay attention to the road. As Mr. Benaiah "Ben" Boyd's lawyer, it is imperative she convinces the judge her client will definitely appear at a motion hearing scheduled for the following week without hinting he is not only out of town but, in a few short minutes, will not be on the planet.

George Lee and Dr. Erica Myers sit on the first row in the master control center at RNR Industries. They, along with Eric Miller, comprised the three-man crew of the *Argo Navis*, the first hyperdrive ship to journey into deep space. General Westbrook of the Space Agency and Professor Hans Mueller, chairman of RNR Industries, have elevated second-row seats in the state-of-the-art new master control center on the campus of RNR Industries, the only publicly known manufacturer of hyperdrive spaceships. Wearing small wireless earpieces to communicate with each other, the third- and top-row flight engineers and the team doctor wait patiently as the computer-generated voice counts down the seconds before the launch of the *Argo Two*, a new hyperdrive spacecraft capable of traveling over ten times the speed of light. Its sole pilot and navigator, Benaiah Boyd, will be making his inaugural flight into space. George, Erica, and the engineers are wearing skintight control gloves to shift around three-dimensional holographic projections. Viewing the launch from his remote location, Eric Miller ultimately has the power to abort the launch.

The spacecraft's destination is a Space Agency–controlled outpost on a border where the original crew of the *Argo Navis* questionably designated a sector of space as off-limits, believing hyperspace travel there zips open space and folds it over our universe. A civilian husband-and-wife team, William and Sarah Davies, is the sole occupant living on the Alpha Station, which is just over ninety billion miles from earth and is the only hyperspace-related project funded by the federal government. The mission of this new ship is to test its maneuverability as well as its pilot's skills. In doing so, it will make a pass around the station and return home. At half the spacecraft's top speed, it will take just under a day to arrive at the station.

The only sounds to be heard in the master control center are the beatings of human hearts. In the midst of various holographic projections opening and closing and moving about, General Westbrook can't help but concentrate on one projection larger than any other and floating high in the air, and it is the view of the spacecraft. In a soft but serious tone while pointing at the screen, General Westbrook asks George, "Is your entire fleet of ships jet-black, son?"

Before George can answer, Grace Gryer, the team doctor, throws a medical monitoring projection above her head by using her right hand and expands it with her left hand for everyone to get a panoramic view. In the middle of the medical projection screen is a detailed outline of a human body, showing blood vessels and vital organs. A smaller graphic in the upper left indicates vital signs. With her left hand's index finger and thumb, Grace Gryer expands the holographic body's heart. Tapping at it with her left hand's index finger, she politely says, "Mr. Boyd's heart rate is extremely high. I think someone needs to say something to him as we are only seconds away from launch."

George Lee taps the side of his left earpiece, opening a channel to the pilot, "Hey, my man. It's G. You ready to do this?"

Five seconds pass, and there is no answer.

"Be there."

The navigational-and-guidance engineer throws one of his 3-D projections of the earth, which was taken from the moon and the width of an entire row, in the air and right above the medical projection. The depth of the projection is not totally realized until a flash of light wisped through the room, causing everyone to duck their heads as if the wave of light was going to hit them. The moon's camera tracks the light as it disappears into space. The navigational engineer minimizes the projection.

"*Argo Two*'s liftoff successful at 10:00 a.m.," reports the flight director.

A few seconds later while the team was still recovering from the spectacular image of the liftoff, a faint message is heard in their ears. "Or B-Square."

The team members look at each other, pondering about the meaning of this message from the *Argo Two*'s pilot.

"Just a little thing Ben and I do," says George. "I say 'Be there,' and he finishes the phrase with 'Or B-Square.' Benaiah Boyd, B-Square, get it?"

After several seconds of blank stares on everyone's faces, George continues, "And yes, General, all our ships are jet-black."

Dr. Myers, the team psychiatrist and navigator on the *Argo Navis*, tosses her own projection for the front-row engineers to see and softly alerts them. "I don't want to burst your bubbles, boys and girls, but the *Argo Two* is spiraling out of control." Using the moon's hyperspace camera, she zooms in on the ship. "You still got a channel open to Mr. Boyd?" she asks George.

Professor Mueller and General Westbrook look at George, well aware of the fact that this is the first solo flight of Benaiah Boyd. George knows, as the pilot of the *Argo Navis*, this new pilot is a natural who picked up on the skill quicker than anyone he had previously trained. Eric Miller trained him in aeronautical and hyperspace-engine engineering and likewise gave him exceptional marks. George is hoping this is not a mistake as he senses that this is what's on General Westbrook's and Professors Mueller's minds. Believing the new pilot has his hands full and not wanting to alarm him, George contacts Ben if for no other reason than to encourage him. "Hey, man. It's G. Just relax and remember your training. Don't overthink the situation. Do what comes natural while using your gloves, hands, and mind to control the ship!"

"That was good, George," admits Dr. Myers, holding her hand over her microphone.

The *Argo Two* is violently vibrating and rolling. Ben knows he is in trouble and franticly struggles to regain his composure. The tumbling motion has caused his earpiece to come out of his ear as well as made him dizzy. He realizes he only has seconds to make corrections or the ship would break apart. Starting to lose consciousness, he forces his right arm forward, activating the glove control. Remembering what George taught him and using his left hand, he painstakingly moves his fingers in a sequence to initiate the ship's stabilizers and inertia dampeners. Not being able to focus on the projection he just opened, Ben grimaces as he attempts to open the ship's pilot projection. "Turn into the roll and slowly straighten out," he murmurs. Closing his eyes, he thinks to himself, *A couple of years ago, I had the chicks, cash, and cars, and now, I'm in this black dish headed for Mars.* He opens his eyes and, with the control gloves and sequence of finger motions, opens the forward viewing portal. Simultaneously he pulls up a 3-D holographic navigational monitor. *Actually, I think I just passed Mars. Oh, what the heck. If I'm going to die, at least I'm saved. Or as Ms. Devereaux tells me, I'm "spared." I like "spared." Man, that's weird too! I never used to think about God before that Holy Ghost hit me. Oh, what the heck. Get it together, man.* The young pilot uses his left hand to open the navigational monitor then slides it to his right. As if he was playing a piano, he opens the ship's main control console. He moves both his hands together and links the two open projections so he can operate the navigational monitor from the main control console. Because his sight has not yet fully cleared, he has a problem with focusing in on the multilayered effects of the projections but is able to open the 3-D representation of the engines. Eric has redesigned this portal so that touching an engine component within the hologram allows the operator to manipulate that component. Ben says out loud in a deep voice imitating Eric, *"Be careful when you use this projection, bro. You can blow yourself up real easily.* Like that is something I'm aiming to do!" Blinking his eyes and focusing on the velocity meter, he notices his speed. "Damn, this thing is fast."

A voice from the main console says, "Eight times light," indicating the ship has now reached a speed of eight times the speed of light.

With his fingers moving through the projections and feeling a bit better, he hears the same voice, this time coming from the navigation projection, say, "Course set for Alpha Station. ETA at present speed—eighteen hours."

Ben gradually reduces the ship's speed and gains control, whispering to himself, "Eric tells me that voice is not Erica's, but I swear he's lying—oops, not supposed to be swearing. Oh well, what the heck. Nobody can hear me." Ben stops for a second and recalls another thing Eric would tell him: *"God hears you."* Ben sits back in his chair, knowing he has brought the spacecraft under control. The anxiety he was experiencing has also subsided. Feeling his ear and realizing the earpiece is not there, he looks down on the deck and grabs it but does not return it to his ear. He closes his eyes, unaware George has been attempting to communicate with him.

In the control center, Dr. Myers announces, "It appears as if Ben has gotten the vessel under control."

"Man, that was close," acknowledges George as he and the other control-room personnel take deep breaths.

"Keep monitoring the situation and trying to reach Mr. Boyd," instructs General Westbrook. "Can I see you in the conference room, Professor?"

As the two men leave the control center, George pats on the seat next to him that was just vacated by General Westbrook, motioning for Erica to sit there. "Are you still planning to take your kids up on the cruise liner?"

"Yeah, George, I am," answers Erica. While shaking her head, she continues, "Why do I get the feeling there is something you want to tell me?"

In a cheerful voice, George replies, "I thought you should know I installed an experiment aboard the cruise vessel. It's Eric's experiment."

"Why is it, George, you seek every opportunity to mention Eric?"

"Because I really do believe you two still have feelings for each other. When is the last time you saw him?"

Removing her earpiece and motioning for George to do the same, Erica answers, "I have not actually seen Eric for over two years since we had our little spat in the hallway after the *Argo Navis's* mission briefing." Then in a calm and subtle voice, she looks directly at George and whispers, "He hypertexted me on the anniversary of my mother's death. Pat Richards told me that you know you're in love with someone when they are constantly on your mind." Looking away from George, Erica admits, "I think of him often but don't know if I should contact him, and if I did, what would I say? What's that mean, George?"

"You tell me. You're the doctor!" suggests George.

"Can you have feelings of love and hate for someone at the same time? What if they both are equally as strong?" After pausing to wipe a tear from her eye, she asks, "So what kind of experiment is it?"

"Let's just say it's a special little room. He has two of them that I know of, the other being in his lab on Ceres. As long as no one enters the one on the cruise liner, everything will be fine. On the first note, the two of you really do need to talk face-to-face and sooner rather than later," suggests George.

In a state-of-the-art conference room adjacent to the control center, General Westbrook pours two cups of coffee, one for himself and the other for Professor Mueller. He hands a cup to his friend, and the two take seats facing each other. "I did not want to say anything in front of the others, but I need you and your staff to keep a close watch on these new recruits. These guys you have trained are not necessarily pillars of society. One problem and the media will be all over it."

Weaving her silver BMW in and out of traffic on Interstate 94 at speeds exceeding ninety miles an hour like a go-kart at an amusement park, Elizabeth Devereaux races to the third district's court in downtown Detroit. Elizabeth removes her satellite-phone headset, having received instructions from Eric. The usually-mild-mannered Devereaux shouts out loud while exiting I-94 and merging onto the Lodge Freeway, "How in the heck did this doggone hearing get moved? Who in their *right mind* would schedule a *blasted* motion hearing for *Friday afternoon at 5:00 p.m.?*" Turning into a downtown parking structure, Elizabeth ponders whether every day of her being a lawyer will be this challenging. She tosses her satellite-phone earpiece into an open briefcase resting on the passenger's seat. Folding down the vanity mirror, she checks her hair and makeup before hastily exiting her vehicle.

The recent University of Michigan law-school graduate has the task of defending a recent RNR Industries intern. Within a year after their maiden voyage in the spaceship *Argo Navis*, George Lee and Eric Miller trained students in antimatter-engine engineering and hyperspace piloting and navigation. The most distinct feature of this institution located at RNR Industries is that all their students are former intercity-gang members. Benaiah

Boyd, whose street name was B-Square, was the leader of a Detroit gang bearing his nickname. B-Square was once heralded as the city's most dangerous gang and had redefined gang activity by becoming RNR Industries' most successful recruits. Today, there are no gangs in Southeastern Michigan involved in criminal activity, and intercity crime is at a historic low. However, some city officials are committed to having these self-rehabilitated criminals answer to their past deeds. Benaiah Boyd is one such person. A motion hearing to dismiss drug-trafficking charges has somehow been mysteriously moved up a week. Elizabeth Devereaux has to convince the judge to adhere to the original hearing date.

Rushing into Judge Wright's chambers, Elizabeth Devereaux, unaware of a gentleman sitting quietly in a dark corner, screams, *"What is going on, Your Honor? Benaiah Boyd's motion hearing is not scheduled until next week!"*

Without looking up at her, Judge Wright reaches over and accepts a letter from the gentleman in his office and hands it to Ms. Devereaux. In a monotone voice and still refusing to look up at her, he replies, "It's not my decision and out of my hands. Where is your client, and how do you plead?"

Opening the letter and acknowledging the well-dressed man in the judge's chambers, she says, "I am not at liberty to say where my client is—"

"Well, you better find out quickly," interrupts Judge Wright while writing on his tablet and still refusing to look Ms. Devereaux in the eye.

Ms. Devereaux excuses herself into the hallway outside Judge Wright's chambers. Installing her satellite-phone earpiece, she initiates a voice command. "Dial Eric Miller."

The satellite-phone system acknowledges with a standard response, "Dialing Eric Miller." After a few seconds, there comes another response. "Unable to contact Eric Miller. Would you like to dial another?"

Elizabeth Devereaux angrily replies, *"Dial Professor Mueller, please."*

"Dialing Professor Hans Mueller."

"Hello," answers Professor Mueller.

"Thank God I reached you, Professor. This is Elizabeth Devereaux, and I need your assistance."

"Good afternoon, Ms. Devereaux. How may I be of assistance?" asks the professor with his native German accent.

After looking around to see if anyone was listening, Elizabeth quietly answers, "A judge is looking for my client Benaiah Boyd. They moved his motion hearing to this afternoon. What should I do? I'm unable to contact Eric Miller."

"Ah, Mr. Boyd—very talented and smart, he is," remarks Professor Mueller. "He should be millions of miles away by now." After a few moments of silence, the professor continues, "Are you still there, Ms. Devereaux?"

"Yes, Professor," acknowledges Elizabeth. "Thanks. That's what I thought. I'll get back to you. Bye now."

Professor Mueller disconnects his headset and looks over to General Westbrook. "That was Ms. Devereaux, and Mr. Boyd has just missed a motion hearing."

General Westbrook, reaffirming his stance, replies, "Like I said, Professor, we have to be very careful with seeing the characters of the men you have trained and now employ. Let Ms. Devereaux handle this matter. She is rather crafty, and there is no need to have the Space Agency publicly involved right now."

Gaining her composure before returning to Judge Wright's chambers, Elizabeth considers establishing a rapport with the men in the room. She ponders saying something like "Boy, who would ever think in a major city like Detroit, three white folks would be considered a minority?" After a few seconds, she realizes how corny that sounds and decides to just tell the truth and pray for mercy. Elizabeth reenters Judge Wright's chambers and announces that her client will not be able to make it to this hearing and politely asks for directions.

Looking up at the young lawyer for the first time and resting his pen, the judge says, "Ms. Devereaux, I do not believe your client is innocent of drug-trafficking and racketeering. This new vocation these thugs have taken up seems to be a convenient cover for their crimes." Pointing to the man in the corner, Judge Wright continues, "Mr. Kennedy and the Feds have only advanced the decision I was intending to make myself. Enter in a guilty plea for drug-trafficking and move on to trail."

"Excuse me, Your Honor, but the purpose of this hearing was to clear my client. There is no evidence he committed any crimes. I motion to dismiss all charges against my client."

Handing Ms. Devereaux a folder, Judge Wright answers, "Motion to dismiss denied. I think I have all the evidence I need. The trial will start a week from today. You have until then to prove the allegations in this jacket wrong. But make no mistake—if proven guilty, I will sentence Mr. Boyd to the maximum amount of time allowed under the law. Good day, Ms. Devereaux."

Elizabeth senses Judge Wright has actually given her an out as the gentleman Judge Wright referred to as Mr. Kennedy reacts to what he just heard by frowning and repositioning himself in his chair. The young lawyer stuffs the legal folder into her briefcase and retreats from Judge Wright's chambers as well as the building as swiftly as she entered but, this time, with a renewed sense of hope.

William and Sarah Davies sit in the drone-control room on the Alpha Station, tracking a deep-space sensor drone. William uses the patented control gloves to operate the drone's propulsion and guidance systems while Sarah monitors the region for space-density changes and any other unusual phenomenon. William carefully accelerates the drone to light speed on the same vector where space folds open. They have been mapping this region to determine the boundaries of the dimensional vortex. Sarah activates a red light on William's holographic console to warn him of an unusual disturbance warranting the drone's return. After months of mapping this region, they have found no end to the phenomenon's event horizon. They have also logged hundreds of unusual effects found within this region not recorded by the *Argo Navis* crew.

Intensely focused on the monitors, Sarah gives her usual instructions to her husband to validate his receipt of her warning. Of all the changes in space-time they have recorded, this one appears to be the most unusual. Sarah asks her husband if he is testing some new maneuver because she is not tracking the drone's return to the station.

With his hands fully extended in front of him and away from Sarah's sight, William initiates a series of finger movements to temporary lock out the gloves' command system. He then brings his arms and hands together and moves his thumbs around each other and replies, "No, dear. I'm just twiddling my thumbs."

"Just as I suspected," says Sarah as she verifies that the uplink to the Space Agency is operational and starts the routine data stream. "Are you monitoring this, Will? Was that some kind of new maneuver, or is this yet another effect we have not cataloged?"

"Yeah, I saw it, but it wasn't me." Unlocking the command system, William explains, "I reset the control system but cannot reestablish navigation or propulsion control. The drone just veered off course like it hit something, and I'm having a heck of a time reestablishing communications."

Sarah opens the station's shutters just in time to visually watch the drone pass the station. At its present speed, it will be out of command range in minutes.

"What the heck just happened, Will?" Sarah rhetorically asks.

"If I didn't know any better, I'd think it hit something. Run a diagnostic on that drone and see if we can gather any information before we lose total communications."

"Starting diag' now," she replies. After shaking her head from side to side, she continues, "This is the first time we have encountered the region appearing to have physical properties. Do you agree?"

William leaves his station and walks over to his companion and stands behind her. He confirms her suspicion and theorizes that this region of space might actually be alive. "As a creature or entity, it might have reacted like we would if an annoying fly kept buzzing around us by taking a swipe at it."

"Do you think we aggravated it?" Sarah asks.

"I'm not sure, Sarah, but let's not move too fast or jump to any conclusions. Let's add this incident to the database and have the computers run an updated analysis." Taking a look at Sarah's telemetry screen, Will notices the drone is several hundred kilometers away and slowing to a stop. "At this distance, the remote control will not work," explains Will.

"Diagnostic's complete, but you better take a look at this," says Sarah. "All drone systems are off-line, and I can't restart the program. Whatever caused the drone to veer off course also disabled it."

Will sits at the console and faces his wife while she moves her chair back a ways from the console to face him. A few seconds pass, and Will suddenly but gently rises out of his chair and trots over to a system log and scrolls through some files.

"What are you doing, Will?" Sarah asks.

"If these logs are correct, RNR Industries will be testing a new ship and plans to fly right around us."

"So you think the new ship hit the drone?"

"No, I don't believe the new ship is in the area yet, nor should it have cloaking technology, even though that would be one explanation. From the logs supplied by the Space Agency, it's not scheduled to be in this area for nearly a day or so. But at faster-than-light speeds, it could be here in a few of hours. What I was thinking is that we could contact the ship and work with the pilot to get the drone back to the station. He might also see something we can't."

Walking over to her husband and grabbing his arm with both her hands and hugging him, Sarah admits, "Oh, Will, now I know why I married you!"

"I have the superior intellect!"

"Heck no, honey. That's not it. You always know how to comfort me and make me feel better."

Will looks back at Sarah in surprise.

"What?" says Sarah with a big smile. "I'll start working on contacting that ship. What is the name of the ship?"

Still with a funny look on his face, he replies, "It's called the *Argo Two*."

Sarah attempts to contact the pilot of the *Argo Two* with no success. She automates the message and sets it to repeat every two minutes. Her message is simple: "We need your assistance." "Let's grab a snack and wait for the *Argo Two* to respond."

Early Friday evening in Houston at the Space Agency, Bill Rogers and David Veil, members of the original *Argo Navis* team, continue to work in their second-floor offices. The old Apollo Mission Control Center was reconstructed to monitor and receive transmissions from the Alpha Station. Analytical data are transferred to Bill Rogers's and David Veil's mobile-satellite computers, eliminating the need to enter the control room. The on-premises mission-control computers keep video logs of the Alpha Station, but these recordings are write-protected to guard the Davieses' privacy. In the event of an emergency, silent alarms will flash throughout the Space Agency, and senior officials will be contacted on their personal satellite-communications systems. In addition, a small amber beacon outside the control room will flash. Therefore, neither Bill Rogers nor David Veil has a reason for working late in the office this Friday. Ironically, the two men leave their offices and meet in the hallway heading to the break room.

"Say, David, what's got you here so late on a Friday evening? Don't tell me you're going to get some coffee so you can work even later!"

"Yeah. I need something to keep me focused, Bill," admits David.

The longtime friends and Space Agency employees engage in petty conversation on their way to the break room. David makes a fresh pot of coffee, and Bill cleans a couple of cups. They take seats around a small dining table, continuing with small talk until the coffee has brewed. Each pours a cup, and instead of returning to their respective offices, they return to sit around the small table. Knowing they are likely the only people, besides the night guard, remaining at the Space Agency, David Veil begins a conversation centered on the Alpha Station.

"I've been reviewing the data streams sent from the Alpha Station, and no two reports are ever the same," cites David Veil. "This region of space is beyond explanation."

"So what type of variances are you seeing?" asks Bill Rogers, who appears to be deeply interested in what his colleague has to offer.

David Veil proceeds by starting with the data-collection drones sent into the region at the exact coordinates and speed the *Argo Navis* entered the region, which formed a destructive tear in the space-time continuum. The custodians of the Alpha Station, cautious of creating another near-catastrophic event, carefully reverse the drones' trajectory. They decided to map the size of the entrance and found the expanse to literally be endless. When they alter the speed at any given entry point, the resulting effects appear to change. By the same token, when a drone enters a specific coordinate at a different time, the resulting effects are different.

David Veil pauses to take a sip of his coffee, giving Bill Rogers time to interject his thoughts. He admits he has been working late hours to analyze the data from the Alpha Station but has different observations. He explains to David Veil that the text accompanying the drones' data are inconsistent. He references an instance logged with a specific log number where the Davieses reported an unusual noise heard throughout the Alpha Station and recorded by the drones upon entering a specific region at a specific time. However, when reviewing the data from that same log number and incident, the drones recorded a spectrum of light, and the Davieses' text observation of the incident confirmed that a blinding light permeated the station through closed shutters.

David Veil picks up the thought from there and asks Bill Rogers if he had time to examine the most recent data received from the station. Bill Rogers nods his head, positively acknowledging David's question. David Veil states that the data from the drone and accompanying text from the Davieses indicate that this particular drone was hit as it entered the region. Both men acknowledge that this seemed to be consistent with their analysis and also note a relatively large energy surge just before the drone entered the phenomenon. This constituted the first time the phenomenon reacted prior to the breach of its space. David Veil and Bill Rogers come to the same conclusion as the Davieses that implied the possibility this phenomenon is living.

"I certainly understand why General Westbrook desires to keep this whole thing guarded," declares Bill Rogers. "If control of this region were in the wrong hands, it could mean destruction for us all."

David Veil leans toward Bill Rogers and, looking Bill straight in his eyes, says, "For some strange reason, I keep thinking about something Eric Miller said, and that is to 'trust your feelings.' By the way, isn't that new ship, the *Argo Two*, scheduled to make its maiden voyage soon and pass close to the station? It would be interesting to know what the pilot observes."

The two scientists wash out their cups and walk out of the break room toward their respective offices. Both agree to call it quits for the weekend. However, as David Veil nears his office, he is surprised to hear his desk phone ring.

"Excuse me for a second, but that ring indicates an inside call." Picking up the receiver, he says, "David Veil speaking."

Pausing and visibly disturbed, he looks at Bill and replies to the caller "Yes, I'll be right down" and hangs up the phone. "That was the security guard at the reception desk. There are a couple of police detectives looking to talk to someone about General Westbrook's administrative assistant, Helen Hayes."

"I'll come down with you!" replies Bill.

Millions of miles from earth, Ben is just reinserting the earpiece back into his ear. In doing so, he picks up a faint message but is unable to hear it. Boosting the signal, placing his hand over his open ear, and squinting his eyes as if it will help, he waits to hear it again but gets nothing. Just as he figures it was all in his mind, a woman's voice startles him. *"Argo Two*, this is the Alpha Station. We need your assistance. Please respond." Believing the message might be automated, he waits for the phrase to repeat. While waiting, Ben reviews his knowledge of the communications system and rehearses a response. "Oh, God, let this be real and not my imagination," he prays to himself. "And guide me through my acknowledgment." He moves the open communications console with his control gloves, placing the holographic display in front of him and making slight movements with his fingers to initiate the sequence that opens a channel to the station.

"Argo Two, this is the Alpha Station. We need your assistance. Please respond."

Very slowly and deliberately positioning his hands and using his fingers, Ben activates the system for two-way communication. In a calm yet concerned tone, he replies, "This is the *Argo Two*. How may I be of assistance?"

Back on the Alpha Station, William and Sarah are in the middle of eating when they hear a voice come from across the room. Both their heart rates rise. The two drop their processed snacks on the table and literally run (if that's possible in a low-gravity environment) to the communication section of the main console. "*Argo Two*, this is Sarah Davies on the Alpha Station. Thanks for acknowledging us. How far away from the station are you?"

"Alpha Station, this is the *Argo Two*. I'll have to calculate my position relative to the station and get back to you. Are you OK?"

"We are fine, *Argo Two*." Smiling and reaching for her husband's hand, Sarah continues, "Who, may I ask, are we speaking to?"

Looking at the navigational projection, he is taken by surprise by the question from Sarah. Thinking as to how he will respond, Ben pauses long enough to cause the Davieses to be concerned. "My name is Benaiah Boyd, but you can call me Ben." Having found the station and his distance from it, Ben cautiously continues, "If I increase my speed, I can be in your area within a few hours. How may I assist you?"

William and Sarah look at each other, not knowing how to describe the problem or how they want Mr. Boyd to assist them.

After a few seconds, Ben starts to think to himself, *My grandmother told me, if it doesn't smell good, don't eat it. And this doesn't smell good.*

William reminds his wife that Mr. Boyd is expecting an answer. "We are not in any danger—just a little something we thought you could assist us with," replies Sarah. "Contact us when you are in range of the station." Then she suddenly severs the communication link.

Ben's uneasiness toward the situation diminishes to the degree that he chuckles to himself. "What kind of games are these folks playing? Is this some kind of test? It's about time I check in with RNR and inform them of the situation." Switching to another wave and setting the power for maximum output, Ben summons the control center. "RNR, this is the *Argo Two*. Do you read me?"

Having not heard from the ship in hours but not wanting to sound overly concerned, George acknowledges, "*Argo Two*, this is RNR. We were wondering how things were going. Are you experiencing communications problems?"

"Hey, G. Good to hear you, brother. Sorry, but I didn't have my earpiece in. But that's not why I'm contacting you. I need your guidance on something."

George mutes his headset and asks for someone to have General Westbrook and Professor Mueller come back into the room. "Hold on just a second, Ben, as I recalibrate the system."

Putting her system on mute, Erica comically replies, "'Recalibrate the system'? Is that the best you could do?"

George shrugs his shoulders and displays a silly little grin on his face. "I guess I'm not good at spur-of-the-moment stuff."

Professor Mueller and General Westbrook hurry into the control room. They pick up their earpieces, place them on mute, and take their seats.

"All set, Ben, so what's going on, my man?" asks George.

"I just got the strangest distress call from the Alpha Station, requesting my assistance. However, when I inquired as to how I could assist, they seemed to play it off and told me they'd get back to me. Are you guys somehow in on this?"

Before George could answer, the general interjects, "Mr. Boyd, this is General Westbrook. I need you to honor their request and assist in whatever way you can. We'll contact the Space Agency and see if they have any knowledge of a situation there. Let us know when you have something more definitive, and we'll let you know what we find out here. RNR out."

Ben scratches his head, convinced they are testing him.

Removing his earpiece, the general requests, "Someone get me David Veil in Houston. It's getting late, so he's probably left the office. Try reaching him on his satellite phone."

After several tries, the communications officer says, "I'm not getting anything, General. I've tried the office and his satellite phone. I've also tried to contact Bill Rogers. Neither man has answered, but I'll keep trying."

"Thank you, son. Let me know the moment you hear anything," replies General Westbrook.

"What do you suspect is going on, General?" asks Professor Mueller.

"I wish I knew, but I got nothing, Professor. I'm curious as to why the custodians of the Alpha Station would contact the ship's pilot before contacting one of us."

Having blown off some steam and asked the Lord for forgiveness, Elizabeth Devereaux arrives at RNR Industries. She plans on being on-site when the *Argo Two* returns home to present the impending bad news to Benaiah Boyd directly. Walking toward the control room gives her a nostalgic and comfortable feeling reminiscent of being in Houston. Running her badge through the access reader, she gets a green light, and the door begins to open.

To her surprise, General Westbrook and Professor Mueller are standing just inside.

Professor Mueller immediately acknowledges her. "Well, hello, Ms. Devereaux. How did it go at the hearing? And by the way, you just missed a call from Mr. Boyd."

Elizabeth walks up to the general and puts both arms around him. With the same height but considerably thinner, she squeezes him to the point that he takes notice.

General Westbrook holds her for a moment and then asks, "Are you OK, Ms. Devereaux?"

Without letting go, she replies, "I'm just thrilled to see a familiar face and be around family." Releasing the general, she gives the professor a smaller hug and tells him, "You folks are all the family I have."

"George, Erica, Grace, and the rest of the team are monitoring the flight. Why don't you join them and take a load off your feet and your mind?" suggests the professor.

"Thanks, Professor. That sounds good. I don't think this day could get any worse."

"We're expecting to hear from Mr. Boyd again soon," says General Westbrook. "Professor Mueller and I are on our way to contact Mr. Veil and Mr. Rogers. Would you like for us to give them a message from you?"

"Sure, General. Tell them I said hello."

Everyone in the control center greets Elizabeth with hugs and kisses. She takes a seat and, within seconds, falls sound asleep. Grace takes off her sweater and drapes it over Elizabeth.

"I need to go home and get some rest myself before tomorrow," says Erica. "The kids will start arriving for the cruise at 6:00 a.m., and I want to be fresh. What time do we launch, George?"

"Liftoff is scheduled for 9:00 a.m. Where have you been staying?"

"I have actually been staying at Eric's house since he's been away."

George sarcastically acknowledges, "'I *see*,' says the blind man."

"It's not like that, George. While Eric's house is big, I would never stay there if it's just him and me. I have a key—just like you do. So why not stay there when I'm in town, seeing I'm here more than in Houston? I'm sure he appreciates someone looking after things until he returns—whenever that is."

"I know, Erica. I miss him too."

"But your relationship is different, George," says Erica as she walks away and leaves RNR's campus.

David Veil and Bill Rogers approach the reception desk, and the night guard points in the direction of the waiting area. David and Bill walk toward two men dressed in suits, who are simultaneously approaching them, and one has his badge in his hand. Holding his gold shield shoulder-high with his left hand and extending his right hand, he introduces himself. "Mr. Veil, I presume? I'm Detective Purkins, and this is my partner, Detective Majours. Is there somewhere we can talk?"

"Right here is fine, Detective. What's going on?"

"Do you know a Helen Hayes?" asks Detective Purkins.

"Yes, sir. She is an employee here. Is she all right?" replies David Veil.

"Not really, Mr. Veil. Earlier today, a jogger reported a woman slumped over in a car. They called police and an ambulance. She was pronounced dead on the scene. The cause of death is still under investigation, but it is believed she suffered a heart attack. We know

23

her identity by her driver's license. A parking sticker in her car window suggests she is an employee here. Not being able to reach a next of kin, we are hoping you can come down to the morgue to make a positive identification."

Shocked by this news, David Veil is speechless, only nodding his head up and down to indicate he will make the identification.

Detective Purkins reaches for a plastic evidence bag being presented to him by his partner. "Among the items on a seat of her car were her purse and these items. Do you recognize these items, Mr. Veil?"

Examining the contents of the bag, David Veil replies, "Yes, Detective Purkins. These are tapes similar to those we use in one of our data-collection-and-monitoring systems. However, I will have to check the index numbers to validate their contents."

Reaching to retrieve the tapes from David Veil, Detective Purkins replies, "Right now, these tapes are evidence in our investigation. Should we determine the death of Ms. Hayes was due to natural causes, we'll make sure they are returned to you." Handing David Veil one of his business cards, he asks to be contacted should anything suspicious turn up.

Suddenly, Bill turns and walks away.

"Where are you going, Bill?" asks David.

"I'm going with you to identify the body!"

"Wait a second and I'll join you," insists David Veil.

Bill stops for a moment, looking at David. "Time's up. You coming?" Again turning and walking away, he shouts, "I'll get your coat and keys, Dave, while you finish up with the detectives." Bill then runs past the elevators and rushes up the stairs.

"Mr. Veil, if you don't mind, I have a couple of questions I'd like to ask you," continues Detective Purkins. "Do you know if Ms. Hayes was seeing anyone or had any close friends?"

"We were her close friends, Detective," interjects David Veil emphatically.

Rushing down the stairs toward the employee-only exit, Bill shouts, "Let's go, David! The night guard will escort the detectives out!"

David Veil hurries to catch up to Bill, who hands him his jacket. Exiting the building, David asks, "You driving, Bill?"

"Yep. I'm right over here," answers Bill, pointing to his car.

The night guard escorts the two detectives out of the building. He casually strolls back to his station and signs them out of the registry. He opens up a book his wife gave him by some new author—Kennis Anthony. She said it is awesome and a must-read. Out of the corner of his eye, he notices a flash. He looks around but sees nothing. The guard reads the index and notices the chapter titles form a poem. Once again, he notices a flash shoot across a wall. He slowly turns the book over and feels for his weapon. As he stands, an amber flash dances across the room. His heart starts to pound as he looks around to determine where the light is coming from. Looking toward the stairway, he notices the light appears to be originating from the second floor. Carefully walking up the stairs with his left hand on his pistol, he follows the light to its source. It is coming from the old mission-control room. He rushes back to his post and retrieves the emergency-procedures manual. He runs his finger down the pages to the latest entry that dictates that he page the mission-control director and then the highest-ranking commander at the facility. Next to these titles are the names of David Veil and General Westbrook. He says a few choice curse words to himself, knowing Mr. Veil had just left the building. He pages him anyway. In seconds, he hears a faint sound coming from the second floor. The guard utters more choice adjectives, this time in sentences, and rushes toward the sound. It was coming from one of the offices. "Don't let this be coming from David Veil's office," he mumbles to himself. Entering David's office, he finds a phone ringing on his desk. This invokes an entire dictionary of foul words from the guard, who hurries back to his post and hopes General Westbrook has his phone as he will call him according to the protocols. Dialing the number given for General Westbrook did not yield an answer, and the guard left no message. To the night guard's surprise, the last instruction in the emergency protocols allows him to clear the alarm, which he happily does and returns to reading his book.

William and Sarah Davies's snack break is cut short when they notice red emergency lights flashing throughout the facility. They hurry to the control room to discover the alarm is originating from the main hangar bay. William turns to his wife to verify if the instruction given to Mr. Boyd was for him to contact them when he was in the area of the station. Before Sarah can answer, the doors to the control room fling open. William looks at the man and says, "You must be Mr. Boyd?"

2. Find a Friend You Can Trust

tanding in a large open living area with a ceiling and walls made of a reddish-colored rock, Eric reminisces on how peaceful this place is. To his right is an open bedroom. To the left of it is a dining area. A smaller room contains cells in the walls storing the by-product energy of a matter-antimatter reaction. Eric has been experimenting on how to use the massive amount of power still radiating from this energy in a transporting device. He created a confinement beam that transports the contents of the small area in the control room to and from two other rooms. One of the two other rooms, located in his home, works fine, but the other room George has installed on a cruise vessel is unable to lock on to any coordinates. Objects can be transported in and out of the room, but the controls on a panel connected to the room cannot sustain stable inbound or outbound transits. Eric believes the problem is related to not having enough stored residual energy coming from the antimatter-reaction chamber. More hyperjumps should correct the problem. Adjacent to the dining area and filling the remaining space carved out of this rock is a laboratory, where a proximity alarm is sounding off. Being in the asteroid belt, Eric does not pay attention to this alert as it sounds frequently due to the movement of floating rocks. While casually strolling over to the console to reset it, he notices an object moving considerably faster than a rock. Not taking the time to sit down at the console, he hurries to identify the object hurling directly toward his position. "That's the *Argo Two*'s signature!" he shouts out loud. He quickly moves to the communications console to open a channel. "Benaiah Boyd, this is Eric Miller. Do you copy?"

To his surprise, a frantic Benaiah Boyd responds immediately. "Copy that, Eric. Sorry for bothering you, but we are in desperate need of your assistance!"

"*We?*" responds Eric in shock. "*You left earth alone!*"

An elderly couple is sitting at a departure gate, waiting for their flight bound for Detroit to leave Houston. They are native Detroiters and enjoy traveling back home to spend time in a house they still own there. The woman, knowing all too well that her husband will not accept the fact that she believes they are being followed, expresses it to him anyway. Her husband of nearly fifty years tells her she constantly gets paranoid when traveling, and she admits that is true. However, she tells her husband the man looks familiar. Her husband smiles, looks over at her, puts his hand on hers, and congratulates her for at least adding a new twist to an old story. She takes her free hand and lays it on top of his then rests her head softly on his shoulder.

Fifty specially selected high school students from all over Southeastern Michigan have arrived at RNR Industries and boarded a cruise liner. The cruise liner is functionally similar to a cruise ship. It was designed to luxuriously carry hundreds of passengers into outer space for a once-in-a-lifetime journey one hundred thousand miles above earth. It has a fuselage over three times the size of a 747 airplane without the wings. There are forty luxury suites, twenty on each side of the ship. Among the amenities are a dining hall and a large viewing room occupying the main level of the cruise liner's bow. The engines and engineering areas are in the ship's stern. A second level running from the ship's stern halfway down the fuselage is the ship's control room. Between the main bridge and the ship's stern is the room Eric Miller has been using for his experiments. Small aisles on both sides of this room allow for access to the engineering areas and the main-level engine room without entering the experiment room. Seven students have been granted special privileges. They will occupy the main bridge and assist George Lee and Erica Myers in the cruise liner's operation. There are no other adults or passengers onboard.

Erica enters the large horseshoe-shaped bridge with her students. There are nine stations, which are basically meant for observation and training, on the bridge. Standing in the rear of the bridge at the heel of the horseshoe is a commander's chair for observation only. Angling out on both sides toward the toes of the shoe are four stations. The top two stations on each side of the toes are the main pilot and navigation stations. George is stationed on the port side of the bridge in the pilot's chair, and Erica will occupy the navigation station across from him on the starboard side.

"OK, young people, as I call your name, take the seat I appoint you," instructs Dr. Erica Myers. "Ion Stein, you will sit behind George Lee. Phair Ghirl, I want you behind Ion. Fashun Maddle, you are behind Phair." While pointing to the position directly behind her navigation station, Erica resumes the seat assignments. "Richard Wright will have the seat directly behind my navigation console. Behind Richard is Dar Skinner. Albie Thayer's behind Dar, and, Albie, take Canta Cee by the arm and escort her to the center chair. We will be preparing for liftoff in ten minutes."

Instead of going to his appointed seat, Ion moves to the seat behind him that was designated for Phair, and while swinging the chair back toward Fashun, he declares, "Uh, Ms. Myers? I feel my extraordinary knowledge and skills would best be appreciated if I sit in front of this beautiful young lady." Looking back at Phair, he continues, "As well as behind the light-skinned Indian babe!"

Moving to the seat intended for her and presently occupied by Ion, Phair insists, "Why don't you just squat down in the seat intended for you? And by the way, I ain't your babe, Einstein."

"First name's Ion. Last name's Stein. Two words," he says, and with a voice like Elvis Presley, he finishes by saying, "Thank you very much!"

Fashun blushes and struts her blond-haired Miss America body to her appointed station and adds, "Now, boys and girls, there's enough of me for everyone."

Albie whispers to Canta as he escorts her to her seat, "It's a good thing you can't see any of this."

"My hearing is just fine," replies Canta as she loses Albie's hand and feels for her seat. "Thank you, Mr. Thayer."

"No problem, Canta. You can depend on me," says Albie.

Having been embarrassed by Phair, Ion takes a peek to see if anyone is still watching him and discovers Dar staring and asks, "Got something to say there, brother?"

The black teenager Dar, not being intimidated by Ion, replies, "I ain't your brother, Einstein."

"Once again, people, first name's Ion. Last name's Stein. *Two words!*"

Standing as if to approach Ion, Dar remarks, "Yeah, whatever, Einstein. I meant to say you act more like Frankenstein—the monster."

"OK, bro, I'll give you that one," says Ion, acknowledging his behavior.

Richard leans over to Dar as both boys take their seats. "Looks like you got the last word, man."

"Yeah. Thanks, man," acknowledges Dar. "So why weren't you on the bus?"

"I live just a few miles away, so my parents drove me here," answers Richard.

"Then we'll have to call you Native Son," explains Dar with a smile, extending his hand to shake Richard's.

Erica claps her hands to get everyone's attention. "OK, *young people*, now that you've got that out of your systems, the next one that acts up or disrespects another will find himself spending the remainder of the trip in one of the suites with the other students." Erica takes her seat and instructs George to prepare for liftoff.

Standing over the body of Helen Hayes after having positively identified her, David Veil is having a hard time believing someone so physically active could have a heart attack. He thinks to himself how she looks as if she is just sleeping and could wake up at any moment. By tightly closing his eyes, David Veil forces tears to run down his face. He silently prays, asking God to give him peace and understanding. A thought also crosses his mind: the region of space his team has been studying is suspected, among other things, to have healing powers. Right now, he wishes Helen Hayes was on the Alpha Station and brought back to life.

Bill Rogers enters the morgue and, upon seeing David with his eyes closed, quietly walks to the opposite side of the table and closes his eyes and says nothing. Moments later, sensing David's movement, Bill opens his eyes and says, "I talked to the coroner who confirms the heart attack. Being a federal employee, they will perform a routine autopsy to verify the cause of death." Bill notices David searching his coat pocket. "What are you looking for, David?" he asks.

"I was wondering why my wife has not called me, seeing it's now Saturday and I have not made it home. I guess I left my phone at the office," declares David.

"Now that you've mentioned it, I don't have my phone either."

David puts his hand on Bill's back as they exit the morgue. "There's a pay phone at the end of the hall. I'm going to stop and give my wife a call. I'll meet you in the car."

"Will do, David," replies Bill, walking past the phone and to the elevators.

David has no children, and his wife does not work on the weekends, so he expects her to be home. The house phone rings just once, and before his wife can get a word out, David starts his dialogue in a defensive tone. "Hi, honey. I'm sorry I'm just now calling you—"

Before he can continue, his wife interrupts him. "David, where in the world are you? I've been so worried. It's all over the news."

"I know, honey. Bill and I have been at the hospital morgue with Helen Hayes."

"*At the hospital with Bill and Helen!*" says his wife. "What's all that got to do with your friends at RNR Industries?"

Surprised by her remarks, David replies, "Helen Hayes had a severe heart attack yesterday and died! What's going on with RNR Industries?"

"*Oh my god!*" cries David's wife over the phone. "That's terrible about Helen. But I'm talking about the explosion of the Alpha Station. They say those people in Michigan that are building ships for you are responsible and are being called terrorists! Tell me you are not involved in that, David."

"*What?*" shouts David, loud enough for the hospital staff nearby to react. "I'm heading back to the agency. I'll call you from there, honey. Love you!"

David hangs up the phone before he can receive a response from his wife. He runs to the elevators and pushes the down button continually for the elevators to arrive; he impatiently runs to the stairs. After opening the door on the main level, the first thing he notices is Bill standing in front of a television set with his eyes and mouth wide open and his hands cuffed together behind his head. Noticing David running his way, Bill turns to speak, but David beats him to the punch. "Come on, Bill. I just found out. We've got to get back to the agency."

As the engineers celebrate the launch of the space liner, Grace Gryer hears someone beating on the outer security door of the control room. The other staff members do not notice her calmly leaving her seat and walking over to see what has someone so outraged. After opening the door, a female employee frantically rushes in, capturing everybody's attention.

"*It's all over the news!*" she shouts. "*Come out here and see,*" she begs.

Professor Mueller and General Westbrook enter the control room, wondering what the ruckus is all about and seeing some of the engineers leaving their posts. General Westbrook yells for everyone to stop.

"Hold on, people," says General Westbrook as he looks at one of the engineers. "Redirect the news broadcast into this room and put it on the monitors." General Westbrook, in his slow yet powerful voice, commands, "Put it on the screen, son."

Everyone quietly focuses their attention on the communications engineer as he works to display a news broadcast.

Having calmed everyone down a bit, General Westbrook motions to have everyone outside the control room to come in.

"I've got it," shouts the engineer as he raises his arm, projecting an image for all to see.

"Recapping this morning's top story, unconfirmed sources within the NIA are reporting that the lone government outpost known as the Alpha Station has been attacked and destroyed. We are switching to our news crews in Detroit where the recently appointed NIA director, William Kennedy, is about to make a statement."

"Good Lord, William Kennedy," acknowledges General Westbrook as he notices the expression on Elizabeth's face as she sees William Kennedy on the newscast.

"Why does that name sound familiar?" asks Professor Mueller.

"It sounds familiar, Professor, because he is the brother of Walter Kennedy. Hold on a minute. I want to hear what he has to say."

"My fellow citizens, at approximately 12:35 a.m., Eastern Standard Time, NORAD's deep-space video scopes captured the images we released to the media that you have undoubtedly seen. While we are desperately attempting to reach the Space Agency for confirmation, we believe there has been a terrorist attack on this outpost and the husband-and-wife team stationed there was killed. The only ships capable of interstellar travel are manufactured by RNR Industries in Ann Arbor, Michigan. Sources have confirmed that RNR Industries had a planned test flight and ship in the area of the Alpha Station when it was destroyed. It is believed that ship was also destroyed in the attack."

Several reporters start shouting, "Mr. Kennedy! Mr. Kennedy! Director Kennedy!"

"I'll take just one question." After pointing to someone he recognized, William Kennedy asked, "Mr. Jenkins, what is your question?"

"Director Kennedy, isn't it possible that a ship in the vicinity of the Alpha Station could have had something to do with its destruction?"

"Excellent question, Mr. Jenkins. If you notice in the video feed, it appears that just before the station was destroyed, an object was seen orbiting the station and was caught up in the explosion. No more questions," says Mr. Kennedy as he exits the podium.

"That was Director Kennedy," says the news anchorman. "Now once more, for those who have not yet seen the video feed—"

"That damn Kennedy," murmurs General Westbrook. "That question was staged."

"Hold on, General. Let's see the video," suggests Professor Mueller.

The entire RNR Industries staff is shocked as their eyes, glued to the monitors, witness what appears to be the Alpha Station along with another image that could possibly be a ship. Seconds later, the object is seen apparently moving from the station very slowly when suddenly, taking everyone by surprise, a thunderous *explosion* destroys them both.

"What's wrong with this picture?" asks Professor Mueller.

"What do you mean?" asks General Westbrook.

"There is no debris," replies one of the engineers. "There is a flash of light, and the Alpha Station just disappears."

"Exactly," admits Professor Mueller. "Has anyone heard from Benaiah Boyd?"

"I'm on it!" shouts one of the engineers.

"What bothers me is how the NIA knows more about this than we do," cites General Westbrook. "They knew the *Argo Two* would be in the area and have deep-space video surveillance of the Alpha Station's alleged destruction. And why haven't we heard anything from Bill Rogers or David Veil? They were supposed to be monitoring the station."

David Veil and Bill Rogers arrive at the Space Agency, and in the rush to exit his car, Bill nearly forgets to put the vehicle into park and turn off the car before leaping out. David has already jumped out a few steps ahead of Bill when he finally parks the car.

Swiping their badges through the reader and entering the building, they are stopped by the night guard informing them of the alarm as they hurried toward the stairs. In a tone and posture worthy of covering his tracks, the guard explains how he followed all the documented protocols and disabled the alarm. David Veil and Bill Rogers thank him for the update and rush up the stairs to the second floor. David Veil heads to his office, securing his satellite phone while Bill Rogers scampers to mission control.

Inside mission control, Bill Rogers heads straight for the video-monitoring system. The first thing he notices is that there are no missing tapes in either the video-storage library or the backup system as he approaches the network-operations center. He logs into the system and accesses the tape logs. David Veil joins him, grasping his satellite phone and confirming the night guard's account of the evening's events. Bill, pointing to the library system, asks David to read off the index numbers on the tapes in the storage library while he checks the electronic numbers in the system. Bill Rogers reads off a number, and David Veil confirms. They do this for several minutes until Bill reads off a number and David asks him to repeat it. Having received a negative acknowledgment from David Veil on three consecutive numbers, Bill replies, "That's what I thought."

"This has something to do with the tapes found with Helen Hayes, doesn't it?" asks David Veil.

Having been standing the whole time, Bill Rogers finally takes a seat and further explains that the tapes currently mounted in the system are blank. The two men spend the next few hours validating the images presented by the NIA to the news media. They both agree it's time to contact General Westbrook.

Bill Rogers and David Veil assemble themselves in Bill's office and open a conference call to RNR Industries, where General Westbrook and Professor Mueller are coming together in the main conference room. Bill starts the conversation, informing General Westbrook that Helen Hayes, the general's secretary for many years, has died and the police are reluctant to rule her death as a result of natural causes. The war-hardened general, holding back his emotions, strongly encourages Bill and David to stay close to the investigation and feel free in using all the Space Agency's resources to aid in discovering the truth. Bill then explains the coincidental discovery of tapes found next to Helen Hayes's body and the suspect destruction of the Alpha Station. Because of the ongoing law-enforcement investigation, the original tapes found with

Helen Hayes remain in police custody. Both Bill and David believe these tapes contain video images of the station leading up to and including its alleged destruction. Bill Rogers adds that the tapes currently mounted in the computerized library do not match the digital index of the tape logs. Furthermore and most importantly, the sizes and properties of the log files indicate the tapes are blank. General Westbrook acknowledges the information given by Bill and David and informs them RNR Industries engineers are desperately attempting to make contact with Benaiah Boyd for his account of the recent events.

Benaiah Boyd skillfully lands the *Argo Two* just feet away from the *Argo Navis* in a landing bay on the asteroid Ceres. Eric is waiting for him at a bay door that resembles a giant garage door. Eric activates a force field and depressurizes the bay, keeping his eye on a pair of indicators—one presently illuminated yellow lamp and one green lamp that indicates the bay is ready to be entered when lit. Within seconds, the green lamp lights up, and Eric rushes toward the *Argo Two* ship with a flatbed cart for a stretcher. The main ramp on the *Argo Two* lowers when Eric reaches the ship and greets Benaiah, who is carrying the bloody body of a woman. It is apparent how much bigger Ben is than Eric as he places the woman on the cart and covers her up. While Eric is turning the cart around to exit the hangar bay, Benaiah speaks up and informs Eric that he will bring the other person. Eric just looks at Benaiah and shakes his head in frustration but wisely holds his tongue and wheels the cart away. Inside his lab, Eric approaches a large black room that appears to have no doors. Looking over his shoulder, he notices Benaiah has caught up with him.

Benaiah notices Eric wave his hand in front of the box and appears to walk right through it. He hears a voice tell him to just keep going straight. The first thing that comes to Benaiah Boyd's mind is when Jesus suddenly entered the room where his disciples were after his resurrection. He dares not think of Eric in the same light. Approaching the large black room, Benaiah closes his eyes and, while carrying the male victim, blindly follows Eric's instruction and enters the room. Once inside, he finds the room has light and Eric has placed his female patient comfortably on the blanket that was covering her.

"She's still got a strong pulse, but we've got to act quickly," insists Eric. "Lay him down next to her," Eric commands.

"I need to talk to you, brother," insists Benaiah.

"I know, big guy, but let us get these two stabilized first. Agreed?"

"Agreed," acknowledges Benaiah Boyd.

Eric then puts his hand on Benaiah's back and compassionately proclaims while he escorts him out of the room, "That new ship must be capable of doing ten times light!"

"Try thirteen," says Benaiah in relief as he is confident he has found a friend he can trust. "So what's the plan, if you don't mind my asking?" insists Benaiah.

Eric retrieves his satellite phone and contacts Grace Gryer at RNR Industries. Upon her answering of her satellite phone, he asks her not to speak. He instructs Grace to go to his home where he will find two patients, one suffering from gunshot wounds requiring immediate attention, and disconnects the transmission. Without an explanation, Grace leaves the campus of RNR Industries, unnoticed.

Eric turns to Benaiah Boyd and compliments him for the excellent job of bandaging the woman's wounds and stopping the bleeding. He realizes Ben has seen his share of gunshots as a former gang member. They swiftly return to the room Eric describes as a transport chamber. He has a similar room inside his home. When Grace arrives, Eric plans to activate the transportation system and send the wounded couple there in the hope that Grace can save their lives.

Benaiah reaches into his pocket and presents a gadget to Eric. Accepting the mechanism and examining it for a few seconds, Eric asks Benaiah Boyd what it is. Without hesitation, Benaiah describes it as a sophisticated receiver used in detonating explosives. He then gives Eric a full synopsis of the events that happened after he left earth until now.

Shaking his head in disbelief, Eric knows the time has come to update Professor Mueller on Benaiah Boyd's whereabouts but not volunteer any more information. Over the years, Professor Mueller has proven to be someone Eric Miller can trust, and he wants to make certain that nothing jeopardizes the safety of the cruise liner, its passengers, and its crew.

David Veil and Bill Rogers are attempting to figure out how the tapes in the secure control room were switched out. The only link to these tapes is Helen Hayes, so they run a report to determine whose badges have accessed the room in the past month. Not to their surprise, Helen Hayes's badge was used every week during the past month and always on a Friday evening. What they discovered next prompted them to contact General Westbrook.

George Lee opens a channel to the communications engineer at RNR Industries, confirming the space liner's readiness to launch. Erica Myers, pointing to her headset, browses her students, verifying that they too have inserted them and are listening to the communications. Erica then gives George a thumbs-up. Everyone on the bridge hears the communications engineer commence a sixty-second countdown to launch. At T minus thirty seconds, George Lee converts the pilot's command console to a holographic display and throws it in front of Ion Stein, instructing him to wave his hand over the launch-sequence section at his command. Ion Stein, along with the other students, put on their membrane control gloves. In a similar fashion, Erica Myers converts her navigation console to a holographic display and, with her right hand, places it between Richard Wright and Dar Skinner. She instructs Richard to wave his hand across the liftoff course and tells Dar to initiate the first program when given the signal. George raises his left hand as the countdown from the engineer reaches T minus five seconds. The soft whisper of the hyperspeed engines is heard as the communications engineer signals to the space liner that it is cleared for launch. George and Erica simultaneously instruct their students to perform the tasks given them. They comply with perfect execution. George Lee opens the front viewing portal, and within seconds, the space liner has reached an altitude of two hundred miles above the earth's surface. Without looking at him and using her ship's communications system, Erica Myers instructs Dar Skinner to execute the first navigation course. Both Erica and George congratulate their students for the professional manner in which they conducted themselves.

Entering the home of Eric Miller, Grace Gryer has no problem with finding the experimental room. She brings out her satellite phone and contacts Eric. "Eric, this is Grace. I'm in position just outside the experimental room. Please advise."

Within seconds, Grace hears a reply from Eric to touch the center of the wall, wait five seconds, and walk into the room right where she will touch it. Grace touches the wall as instructed, but nothing happens. She counts for five seconds and, with blind faith, proceeds straight into the wall. To her surprise and delight, she enters the cubicle and finds the room dimly lit. She looks behind her and finds no indication of a door, yet straight ahead are the bodies of a man and a woman. She rushes toward them and, while kneeling between them, checks for pulses. Both are alive. Using her satellite phone, Grace calls a friend who operates an EMS bus. She plans to take the couple to a private clinic for treatment, praying it will not be too late.

Sitting in first class on a flight from Houston to Detroit allows a man to be one of the first to disembark the aircraft. Finding a phone booth, he takes a seat and retrieves a satellite phone from the inside pocket of his sports coat. He uses voice commands to dial a director. The man on the other end recognizes the number and therefore does not speak to acknowledge the connection. The man at the airport announces he is in town. The man on the other end is surprised to hear this and pauses several seconds before requesting the man at the airport to meet him at a downtown-Detroit bar and rudely disconnecting the call. The man at the airport removes the phone from his ear and glances at it briefly before returning it to his pocket. He watches as an elderly couple walk past, unaware of his presence.

3. HATRED YOU CAN'T CONCEIVE

P rofessor Mueller and General Westbrook have assembled all the employees of RNR Industries in the executive conference room. General Westbrook looks over the audience and asks if anyone had seen Grace Gryer. The communications officer believes she had left the campus. General Westbrook thanks him and proceeds by telling his audience that he is not a praying man but wanted Grace to lead them in prayer because he believes evil is ever present and it will take divine intervention to prevent the forces of evil from prevailing. The reason he had assembled them together is to explain what he believes is hatred that is hard to conceive and the nemesis behind it. He wants them to be aware of it as their lives could all be in grave danger. He brings to their remembrance the former NIA director, Walter Kennedy. They were all around a few years ago when his attempt to build and launch the first hyperspace vessel based on schematics he stole from Eric Miller's project cost him his life. He reminds them that the region of space they are guarding and studying is capable of destroying our solar system when folded open by hyperspace travel. There are others who believe this region of space has life-sustaining properties and are obsessed with gaining control of it. The most vocal ringleader of this circus is the new NIA director, William

Kennedy. He is the brother of the former NIA director, Walter Kennedy, whom they all knew. In the days to come, they will no doubt hear negative reports about RNR Industries' operations. Therefore, they need to diligently and meticulously piece together the facts surrounding the events of today relative to the Alpha Station. And by all means, they must not let anyone discourage them or listen to any reports that label them as anything but the honorable and outstanding scientists and engineers they are.

General Westbrook pauses for a few seconds before raising his head and looking in the direction of Elizabeth Devereaux. "David Veil and Bill Rogers informed me that sometime yesterday, Helen Hayes, my secretary for many years, had passed away. The exact cause of her death has not yet been confirmed, but it appears she suffered a massive heart attack and died in her car. There is currently no connection between her death and the events at the Alpha Station. Professor Mueller and I will contact George Lee and Erica Myers on the cruise liner as well as Eric Miller, who is somewhere in the asteroid belt. We all have duties to perform, and I'm expecting nothing but the professionalism and expertise you have demonstrated in the past becoming the catalysts for our future successes. Are there any questions?"

Elizabeth Devereaux tries to hold back the tears, but when General Westbrook approaches her, she collapses in his arms. Some in the room come over to assist Elizabeth, knowing she and Helen were close friends.

Professor Mueller informs his staff that it is the weekend and none of them are expected to stay. He understands if they want to go home to their families, but not one soul leaves the premises. Everyone returns to their assigned duties.

Professor Mueller's satellite phone signals an incoming call. Noticing the caller ID is that of Eric Miller, he excuses himself to the smaller meeting room adjacent to the main conference room. Eric informs Professor Mueller that Benaiah Boyd is alive but the remainder of what he has to say is speculative and must be kept between the two of them. Before ending the call, Eric tells Professor Mueller it is necessary to share what he said with George Lee and Erica Myers on board the cruise liner as their lives could potentially be in danger.

Continuing to embrace General Westbrook in the main conference room but composed enough to speak, Elizabeth quietly reveals there was a man in Judge Wright's chambers whom she is certain was William Kennedy.

Outside the Detroit Metropolitan Airport, a very well-dressed man carrying only a leather briefcase hails the next available luxury limousine. The approaching black Cadillac DeVille stops. The driver exits the vehicle, opens the rear side door, and welcomes his fare to Southeastern Michigan. Closing the door after the gentleman is comfortably seated, the chauffeur hastens to his driver's seat, closes his door, and just before setting the meter, goes through his normal routine to make his passenger feel comfortable.

"Welcome again to Detroit, sir. My name is J. F. Jones, but you may call me JF. Where can I take you today?"

"Westin Hotel in downtown Detroit" is his passenger's sharp response.

"Right away, sir," states JF, who senses this trip will be without much conversation. However, he feels it is not polite to not at least attempt to be friendly as tips are a major part of his compensation.

"Where are you arriving from?" he asks as he looks in the rearview mirror with a smile at his customer.

"Spare me your chivalrous remarks and just drive," insists the man.

Without question, J. F. Jones takes his passenger's advice. Upon arriving at the hotel, the driver checks the meter, but his passenger, having already seen the fare, throws just enough to cover the cost on the front seat and exits the car without closing the door. J. F. Jones exits his vehicle and circles to the other side to close the side door, and he can't help overhearing his discourteous customer asking someone on the other end of his phone for his room number.

The man in the hotel room quickly disconnects the call and, using a speed-dialing system, connects to another party. All the man in the hotel room says when the other party answers is that he has a job for them. "Take out a man who will be waiting at the Midtown Restaurant, and be sure you are seen wearing the jackets supplied." He ends the call by telling the assassins that the intended target will actually call them.

Entering the Westin Hotel, the rude man goes directly to the elevators without acknowledging anyone, waits for an elevator car he can occupy alone, and proceeds to the floor connected with the room number. A quarter of the way down the circular hallway, he stops, looks around to see if anyone had noticed him, and knocks once on the door. Another well-dressed man opens the door, invites him into the room, and asks that he close the door behind him.

"How was the trip from Houston?" asks the man occupying the room.

"It was without incident, Mr. Kennedy," replies his guest.

"Interesting. You say 'Without incident'?" suggests William Kennedy. "What do you call the couple on the plane?"

"I will take care of them," replies the man.

"Of course you will," interjects Mr. Kennedy. "You must be hungry. Let's grab a bite to eat. There are some excellent restaurants in this town that stay open late. I'll meet you at the Midtown Restaurant in an hour to discuss your next assignment." Mr. Kennedy asks the man to give him his phone in exchange for another one he is handing him. He instructs the man to call the preprogrammed number once he arrives at the restaurant. Mr. Kennedy then escorts the man to the door.

Traffic is unusually light during J. F. Jones's return to the airport. He happens to be the next available luxury car for hire as he approaches the curbside service lanes. Noticing an elderly couple attempting to cross the street to head for the taxis, his heart leads him to offer them his service. Pulling his limousine in front of them and prohibiting them from crossing the street, he stops and quickly exits his vehicle. The couple becomes frightened by his actions, but he calms their fears with his pleasant personality.

"You two youngsters appear to be in need of comfortable transportation," insists J. F. Jones. Opening the right rear-side door and assisting them with their baggage, he continues, "And I am just the right person to supply it."

"I'm sorry, but we can't afford to have you take us all the way to Ann Arbor," says the elderly female.

"I always charge Wolverine fans a flat twenty dollars," explains J. F. Jones. "So you really can't afford to turn this down."

"So what're you waiting for, son? Go Blue!" cries the elderly gentleman as he assists his wife into the car.

J. F. Jones enters the vehicle and asks them for their destination. They give him the address to a home they own in northwest Ann

Arbor known as Auburn Hills. They tell him a young lady they knew in Houston who moved to Ann Arbor to become a lawyer is interested in purchasing the property. They have returned in hopes of finalizing that deal. J. F. Jones is acquainted with the area and knows it is a wealthy community. He tells them he could not help but notice one of their expensive suitcases seemed to be damaged. The couple spends the entire trip explaining how they have spent the past few hours filing a baggage claim. Upon arriving at their destination, true to his word, J. F. Jones only charges the couple twenty dollars even though he believes they could pay much more. He assists them with their belongings and leaves them a business card, instructing them to call him should they need his services in the future.

William Kennedy's associate arrives at a Detroit restaurant and requests a private table. He informs the hostess he will have a guest arriving soon and only orders a beer. Soon after, a waitress arrives with his beer and asks if he wants to view a menu. He somewhat-rudely responds that she obviously did not hear him, so the waitress leaves. The man retrieves the phone William Kennedy gave him and dials the preprogrammed number. One of two men sitting at the bar, both wearing jackets with large "B-Square Detroit" insignias on the backs, answers the phone while the other man looks around to see who is talking. The second man taps the man with the phone in his hand, and they walk over to the booth where William Kennedy's associate is sitting and says, "Yeah? You ring?"

William Kennedy's associate looks up with surprise and reaches down to his side to access a loaded handgun, but the second man has taken a seat next to him and says "Not so fast, big guy!" and takes away his weapon.

William Kennedy's associate calmly informs them that he is a federally sanctioned assassin currently on an assignment. The first man with the phone responds that so is he. He then asks the federally sanctioned assassin to quietly follow him and his partner outside. William Kennedy's associate smiles as he feels he will be able to overtake his would-be attackers outside the restaurant. The three men exit the restaurant with William Kennedy's associate sandwiched between the other two. While the second man opens the door to a parked car, William Kennedy's associate strikes him hard with a karate chop to his throat. However, the first man behind him pulls out a twelve-inch knife and stabs him several times in the back. William Kennedy's associate falls with his back to the car and, with all the strength he has, attempts to grab the knife from the first attacker, but he is too strong and stabs the federal assassin two more times in the stomach and pushes him onto the backseat of the car. Recovering from the blow to his throat, the second man rushes to the driver's side of the car. The first man, now in the backseat of the car, closes his door and instructs the driver to slowly pull off. The first man puts some papers in the coat pocket of his victim along with the knife he used to kill him. They drive to an east-side Detroit neighborhood that was once the territory of the B-Square street gang and dump the body of William Kennedy's associate in an alley.

William Kennedy's satellite phone rings while he sits at a desk in his downtown-Detroit hotel room. He answers the incoming call by saying hello. The caller on the other end responds by saying he is in place and eager to carry out his next assignment. William Kennedy acknowledges by instructing the caller to await his next orders. Disconnecting the call and returning to his computer, he accesses a secure airline database. He searches for a flight originating in Houston that was bound for Detroit. Finding the same flight his earlier visitor was on, he accesses the flight manifesto to find couples. With that information, he uses his security-level credentials to access another database of civilians that, in particular, has those couples on the flight who have roots in Houston and Detroit. To his surprise, he found only one elderly couple. He thinks to himself how easy that was and adds their Ann Arbor address to a text message on a disposable phone that began with the phrase "This is your next assignment."

Bill Rogers and David Veil believe they can be of greater assistance to the team at RNR Industries by being there with them. They have installed remote-access protocols to all the systems at the Space Agency and are heading to Ann Arbor to join their colleagues. David Veil contacts Detective Purkins, informing him of their journey to the Detroit area should he need to contact them.

Sleeping quietly on a recliner nested between the beds of William and Sarah Davies, Grace Gryer is awakened by a soft touch on her shoulder. She looks over her shoulder to notice it is the hand of William Davies. Grace rises from her chair to William's side. Lying motionless with his eyes closed, he asks who she was and about his wife, Sarah. Grace introduces herself and tells him Sarah is lying on a bed on the other side of her chair and is expected, like him, to be all right. William slowly turns his head to verify the woman's statement. He thanks Grace and falls back to sleep. Grace picks up her satellite phone to inform Eric Miller of the Davieses' conditions and that she will soon be returning to the campus of RNR Industries.

On the asteroid Ceres, Eric Miller acknowledges Grace Gryer's messages. Standing next to Eric is Benaiah Boyd anxiously awaiting news of the Davieses' conditions. Eric puts his hand on Benaiah Boyd's shoulder and informs him the Davieses are going to survive. Benaiah drops to his knees and begins to thank God for sparing the Davieses' lives.

Erica Myers has spent much of her time with the forty guest honor students on board the cruise liner. What she expected to be an entertaining conversation about the cruise liner's design and operations and her students' knowledge of outer space was far from their minds. Instead, she has managed to break up a brawl between several students from affluent families and school districts claiming they have more of a right to be on board the cruise liner than students from financially distressed social backgrounds and school systems. Not surprising, the majority-ruling inner-city kids who did not take kindly these allegations were well able to defend themselves and their cause. Having directed the disenfranchised students not to reenter the lounge where they were all gathered, Erica told them they still had freedom to browse the ship. However, for the handful of other students who looked down on them, she has restricted their access to the ship and they must spend the remainder of their stay locked down in the lounge. In a private conversation with them, she could not convince them of their error and realized they had a hatred she could not conceive. Exiting the lounge, Erica heads back to the main bridge. Upon her arrival, she notices George Lee hovering over the seat of Dar Skinner at the navigation console. She approaches them and, while standing next to George, asks what they are doing, praying these specially selected students are not having the same issues as the other forty.

"Hey, Doc," replies George. "Dar has detected an unusual signature off our starboard side. You returned at a good time as he is suggesting we alter our orbit to see how the energy reacts. Richard and Dar have plotted a small course correction."

Dar Skinner looks back at them and asks Erica if she wouldn't mind checking their work. Erica returns to her main navigation console and states, "So it seems like you guys have been busy!"

"*And girls,*" immediately reply Canta Cee and Phair Ghirl in unison. "It was Canta who assisted Albie in isolating the ship's energy signature from the outside of the ship," insists Phair. And after winking at Ion, she continues, "And Einstein and I are prepared to execute the navigational change provided by Dar and Richard. George has also verified this is not an energy produced by RNR Industries–built vessels, so there is nothing wrong with this ship."

"Very well, team," says Erica, correcting herself. "What do you think, George? Should we contact RNR and let them know what we are doing?"

"As the communications officer, Fashun is keeping a ship's log. Let's exercise this maneuver and see what happens. It could be nothing, so let's not alarm anyone until we have something more definitive. We don't want General Westbrook and Professor Mueller to accuse us of reacting to the concerns of our students."

"Very well, George. In the words of an infamous starship captain, *engage!*"

The students under the guidance of Erica Myers and George Lee execute their planned maneuvers. With Canta's assistance, Albie verifies the energy signature is no longer alongside the vessel. The students start to formulate their opinions, but George insists they continue to monitor the exterior of the vessel and let him know should the energy signature return.

George Lee and Erica Myers are watching their bridge-selected students mature, allowing them to engage and control the vessel's operation. Ion Stein and Phair Ghirl pilot the vessel under George's watchful eye. Richard Wright and Dar Skinner navigate and execute the course corrections Erica had preprogrammed at their consoles. Albie Thayer escorts Canta Cee to the engineering level as she is an avid student of advanced engineering technology. Fashun Maddle escorts Dr. Myers as they check on the students given freedom to roam the remaining sections of the cruise liner. To Erica's surprise, the thirty students have assembled themselves in the aft viewing lounge, discussing social-behavior sciences and the selection process for future crews. Dr. Myers and Fashun Maddle join in the conversation, delighted by the fact that they have determined to use the incident with the prejudiced students to broaden their understanding of the importance of screening in the crew-selection process. After the discussion, Dr. Myers approves their desire to share their findings with the isolated students in the main lounge and applauds their desire to put aside their differences and be the olive branch for peace.

Dr. Erica Myers and Fashun Maddle are walking slowly back to the bridge when Fashun stops and asks her if she can have a couple of minutes alone. "Dr. Myers, I want you to know how much I respect your work as a scientist, navigator, and doctor," explains Fashun. "I'm really not just some dumb blond like some people think when they see me or before they get to know me. In fact, I have a language-translation device that works better than the ones in the market today." Reaching into her pocket and handing the device to Dr. Myers, she says, "It would really be an honor for me if you were to take a look at it and tell me what you think."

In an attempt to be courteous, Dr. Myers receives the device and responds, "You know, Fashun, there and many universal translators in the market today. What distinguishes yours from the others?"

Excited by Dr. Myers's response, Fashun moves in front of Erica and says, "I'm so glad you asked, Dr. Myers. My device not only translates languages not used anymore, like Latin, but also attempts to incorporate slang words and profanities." Noticing Dr. Myers is somewhat uninterested, Fashun elaborates, "What I mean, Dr. Myers, is that my device gives a more accurate translation—"

"No need to explain, Fashun," interrupts Dr. Myers. "Maybe I'll test it out on George and give you some feedback."

Continuing on toward the bridge, Fashun begins another conversation. "Do you mind if I ask you something personal, Dr. Myers? And you do not have to answer if you don't want to, but is it possible for someone to love someone and hate them at the same time? I mean, can you have both these feelings for the same person?"

This time, Dr. Myers is the one who stops and, looking Fashun right in the eyes, turns a question back on her with an exploratory question of her own. "Why do you ask, Fashun? You seem kind of young to be experiencing these kinds of mixed emotions."

"Well, I know you are a psychiatrist, Dr. Myers, and there is this guy at school who I really like, but sometimes he drives me absolutely nuts!"

Somewhat relieved that Fashun was not inquiring about her relationship with Eric Miller, Dr. Myers puts her arm around Fashun and, while resuming their walk toward the bridge, explains, "Women just happen to bring out the best and worst in men, my dear!"

As they continue their walk, Dr. Myers discovers that Fashun's mother had passed away and she is really in need of a mother figure, something Dr. Myers can relate to. She promises Fashun that she will be available for her whenever she needs it. Arriving at the bridge, Fashun gives Dr. Myers a long, tight hug, and the two return to their stations.

Meanwhile, Ion and Phair have done some bonding of their own. Phair admits to her bridge partner, "You know, Ion, when we first got underway, I really thought I was going to hate you, but you are not that bad a guy. I have learned a lot from you in the past few hours. Thanks for keeping me as your partner."

"*Hate* is a pretty strong word, Phair," admits Ion as he looks over at Phair and ceases from working the holographic controls. "I have a tendency to mess with people of all nationalities and creeds, but I do not *hate* anyone. Sometimes it's hard for me to conceive just how much hatred there is in the world today." While continuing to open and close various holographic windows within the pilot's console, he admits, "I first thought you were just letting me take control of the consoles because you were afraid I might insult you." Then smiling, he continues, "And if that is not true, let's just pretend that it is!" Then stretching out his arm toward Phair, they shake hands.

On the other side of the bridge, Dar and Richard are having a similar type of bonding experience. Dar tells Richard his parents could never afford to send him on this kind of adventure. If it were not for his grades and interest in science and astronomy, he would not be here. Then he asks Richard, "How did you come about this opportunity?"

Richard responds bluntly, "My father is a judge in Wayne County, serving some district in Detroit. I think he paid for me to be here." Then recognizing what he just said in light of how Dar got here, he stops pulling up star charts and apologizes. "I don't think that came out right, Dar. I'm sorry!"

"Not a problem, Native Son!" says Dar with a smile.

"Believe it or not, I read that book," admits Richard. "I was playing around on the web one day, searching for men who had the same name as me, and discovered the author. It is a great book. I don't expect you to understand, but I sympathize and relate to Bigger Thomas. And for what it's worth, I've seen you navigate through these star charts like it was second nature. You deserve to be here a lot more than I do, Dar."

"Thanks. I appreciate that, Bigger—*oh*, I mean Richard," jokes Dar.

Communicating to each other through their communication earpieces so the students on the bridge wouldn't be alarmed, Erica whispers to George, "I'm getting an incoming message from an unidentified source. Can you confirm?"

"I see it too, Erica, but it is not unidentifiable. This signature is from the Ceres Asteroid. Eric Miller is on Ceres!" notes George. "I'm patching it through."

"Cruise Liner, this is Eric Miller on Ceres. Do you copy?"

"So that is where he is!" says Erica, looking toward George with a smile.

George smiles and asks, "Do you want to respond, my dear?"

"*Oh!* May I, George? But you might want to pull off your headset," replies Erica in a jovial voice.

Not sure how much Erica is really teasing him, George mutes his headset and informs Dr. Myers he is going to check on Albie and Canta in engineering.

As Erica watches George leave, she realizes this will be her first voice-to-voice conversation with Eric in roughly two years and is curiously excited about it. She takes a deep breath and responds to his hail. "This is Dr. Erica Myers on the cruise liner. Go ahead, Eric."

After what appears to be an eternity, Eric replies in a low voice, not knowing if George is listening, "Oh, Dr. Myers, I can't tell you how pleasant it is to hear your voice. It has been a long time." Eric pauses, awaiting Erica's reply and believing it was his remarks that caused Erica to push back on their relationship.

He has had nearly two years to dwell on the fact that witnessing to someone who is not familiar with the Bible takes patience. He realizes how hard it is especially if one loves them. But he must give her time to embrace it for herself and not because of a selfish desire for her to be equally yoked in the same faith, not to mention he never told her how he truly felt about her. In his spirit, he prays her next remarks will give him the sense that what he believed he had broken can be mended.

On the other hand, Erica feels as if it was her fault that things ended on an unpleasant note. She is not sure Eric loves her in the same way she loves him. She is cognizant of the fact she cannot push him to disclose his feelings for her and wants to learn more about his religion. Knowing he is waiting for her acknowledgment, she wants to let him know, even if by no more than the tone in her voice, that she wants to reconcile with him.

"I know it has been a long time, Eric, and I've missed you. It is so good to finally hear your voice. What can we do for you?"

Getting the response he was anticipating, Eric knows he has to get to the real issues they are facing. "I'm not sure you are aware, Dr. Myers, but I have an experimental room on your cruise liner."

Erica cordially replies, "Yes, I am. Go ahead."

"That room is a portal chamber. There are three of them: one on the cruise liner, one here inside the asteroid, and another in my home on earth. All three can be linked together but only two at a time. The residual by-product of the hyperspace engines powers each room. The power of any one room once linked to another will power that other room as well. I can monitor conditions in each room from my console on Ceres. Objects entering in each room automatically activate a room-ready condition. Right now, I'm reading at least one or more objects in the cruise liner's room. If you would not mind, I'd like for either you or George to check it out. It could be just a faulty sensor."

"Will do, Eric," replies Erica. "And for the record, George dropped off the line just after you contacted us. He is presently in engineering now. We'll check it out and get back to you. Dr. Myers out."

Back on the Ceres Asteroid, Eric notices that the room on the cruise liner was just activated. It was last linked to the room at his home, and he trusts that condition was not altered. He begins to get nervous, but Benaiah Boyd settles him down by encouraging him to wait for a reply from Dr. Myers.

Erica informs the bridge crew they will be on their own while she and George are in engineering. On her way to engineering, Erica feels better than she has been in years. However, as she approaches the room, she notices George standing outside the room with his hands on his head and talking to Canta and Albie. Just on the other side of the room, she hears a voice familiar to that of the student who was causing all the ruckus in the main lounge.

"What's happening, George? And why are you guys along with Mr. Temper staring at a black wall?" asks Erica.

George stretches out his hand as if to touch the wall, activating the door to the room. Apparently, Canta figured out this room was a portal and had explained this to the students before he arrived and that they should exit it. He tells Erica that just before she arrived, Mr. Temper was in the room with the forty students but hastened out when he arrived, hitting the side of the room hard enough to activate the control panel. Erica looks in the direction of George's hand but cannot see anything.

"What are you talking about, George? The room is dark and appears to be empty," suggests Erica.

"Exactly," submits George. "When this butthead hit the wall and activated the controls, the students inside the room disappeared."

Erica walks just inside the room, activating the faulty control panel. Gotta Temper begins to follow her, but George pulls him back. In a rage, Mr. Temper strikes the control panel, and the display goes to zero and starts incrementing. Then the power to the room and the control panel shut down, sealing the entrance to the room with Dr. Myers in it. In his rage, George karate-chops Gotta Temper in his throat, knocking him to the deck. George picks him up, drags him to a nearby guest cabin, and locks him in. He then demands Canta and Albie follow him to the bridge.

On the bridge, George frantically opens a channel to Eric. The junior bridge crew asks where Dr. Myers is, but Albie shakes his head, indicating they should be quiet. With a channel now open to Eric, George explains the situation to him, not concerned that the young bridge crew can hear their conversation. He also avoids telling Eric, who has been monitoring the situation, that

Erica is the person trapped in the room. Eric tells George they need to generate residual energy from the hyperspace engines in order to generate enough power to reactivate the room. George tells him that it could take several minutes to fire up the engines. Eric tells him someone will have to divert the residual energy from containment to the room. George tells Eric he is not sure he knows how to do that, but before Eric can respond, he hears someone say to George, "I believe I can do that, Mr. Lee."

"Who was that, George?" asks Eric.

"That, Eric, was one of our students, Canta Cee," replies George as Eric also hears him remind Canta that she is blind.

"Yes, Mr. Lee, but Albie will be my eyes," insists Canta.

"How do you know all this, Canta?" asks George.

"Don't forget I'm an engineering scholar, Mr. Lee. I have been following Eric Miller's works for a couple of years, and I believe I know this system. Albie can assist me, sir. Please let me help," begs Canta. "I feel partially responsible for Dr. Myers being locked in that room."

"Erica is in the room, George?" shouts Eric.

Eric asks Canta and Albie to go to engineering and explains to them where to find the holographic-control gloves. The gloves will allow them to open a communications console linked to the bridge so he will be able to converse with them as well as the bridge crew.

As Canta and Albie rush off to engineering, George shouts over to Richard and Dar, urging them to find warp-speed navigational courses near an earth origin while explaining to Phair and Ion how to pilot the ship in conjunction with course settings coming from Richard and Dar. Before leaving the bridge, he puts Fashun in charge and tells them to listen to instructions on the open communications channel from himself and Eric. He will be in the lower engineering level, attempting to route residual energy from the engines directly to the test room. George encourages them to be strong as he knows he is asking a lot from them but has faith that they will embrace the challenge.

Eric Miller instructs Benaiah Boyd to prepare the *Argo Two* for liftoff in case he is needed to assist the cruise liner. With all channels open, he receives a message from George that he is in position in lower engineering and waiting for Eric's instructions. Canta and Albie likewise report that they are ready. Finally, Fashun yells out from the bridge that Richard and Dar have found and plotted a course that will take the ship past the moon and away from the planets and the sun. Ion and Phair are prepared to execute the course at the speed of light to prolong the journey and build up enough residual energy to free Dr. Myers. Eric acknowledges the bridge crew and asks Fashun to start a thirty-second countdown till execution. Eric then instructs George to monitor the containment flow. The containment chambers need to be at 25 percent before he can start manually diverting energy to the room. Too much flow to the room could cause problems Eric cannot predict. Finally, Eric instructs Albie to let Canta know when the room starts to receive power. The experimental-room systems will need to be fully charged before Canta will be able to determine the condition of the room.

Fashun counts down from ten seconds, holding her right hand in the air. With their eyes on her, Phair and Ion signal they are ready. After counting to three then two then one, Fashun lowers her right hand and, while pointing in the direction of Ion and Phair, says just one word: "Execute."

Ion tells Phair that the engines are online and she can start to increase their speed according to the parameters set by the course Richard and Dar have provided. Moving her hand over the pilot's speed controls, she counts off the increments of velocity leading up to warp speed.

Seeing the cruise liner slowly moving toward the moon, a soldier opens a channel to William Kennedy. "The cruise liner is starting to move toward the moon, sir," he says.

William Kennedy acknowledges the soldier and thanks him for his duty. As the soldier contemplates the words spoken by Mr. Kennedy, he is jolted back into his chair as his vessel starts to move on its own despite his efforts to control it.

J. F. Jones returns to the airport. Offering to take that elderly couple to Ann Arbor was a kind gesture, but it cost him two hours' worth of fares. When he would normally retire for the evening, he wants to attempt to pick up at least one more run. But at this time of the evening, flights are few and far between, and so is business. Pulling into the limo lane, there is one car ahead of him. He thinks to himself how wonderful it would be if that driver called it a night and left him next in line. To J. F. Jones's delight, he notices the brake lights illuminate and the car slowly moving forward. What he did not notice was the driver moving ahead to load his next fare. Jones then debates how much stopping for gas might have cost him. Nevertheless, he advances to the first spot and shuts off his engine. Checking his watch, the past fifteen minutes seem more like fifteen hours. While debating whether to call it quits for the night, he notices headlights shining in his rearview mirror. Another limousine is pulling in to line behind him. *What are the chances,* he thinks to himself, *I will pull off empty and this guy gets a two-hour run?* So J. F. Jones sits, patiently watching the second hand on his analog watch slowly circle the clock's face. Then suddenly, the headlights on the limo behind him catch his attention, but the car does not move. He then notices two men walking out of the terminal. If he had checked the arrival board, he would have realized a late incoming flight from Houston. He thanks God for the potential fare, starts the vehicle, and pulls up to greet them.

J. F. Jones pops open the trunk as he exits his luxury sedan. "Welcome to Detroit. My name is J. F. Jones. Where can I take you, gentlemen?"

"Thank you, Mr. Jones," says one of the men loading his luggage and what appears to be some other equipment. "We are heading to Ann Arbor, but can you recommend a good coffee shop in the area we can stop at first? I am literally dying for a cup of java."

"Not a problem, sir. There is a good place I recommend just outside the airport. Where in Ann Arbor are you heading?" asks the limo driver as he begins to pull off.

"We are going to a laboratory-and-manufacturing campus known as RNR Industries. We have an address if you need to plug it into your GPS."

"No need for that," replies the limo driver. "I am familiar with that facility. An old acquaintance of mine is employed there."

Minutes later, they hear J. F. Jones declare, "Here we are, gentlemen—the best coffee this side of midnight. I will suspend the meter until we get back on the road."

"Much appreciated, Mr. Jones," says the gentleman doing all the talking. "We'll only be a minute."

Just minutes after entering the store, his two passengers exit with their beverages. J. F. Jones also notices two young men who appear to be wearing B-Square gang jackets, but he cannot be certain because his passengers are holding the door for them and blocking his view. When his passengers enter the vehicle, the quiet one whispers to the other that those two young men were very nasty. J. F. Jones also hears the other man comment that one of them also deliberately bumped into him as if to insight a confrontation. J. F. Jones inconspicuously pretends to be editing his logbook but is really waiting for the pair to exit the building so he can get a better look at them. Peeking up with his eyes with his head down toward his journal, Jones cannot determine if there are any other customers in the store or the location of the young men. Suddenly, gunshots erupt, and the two young men run out of the store, shouting that the place was hit by the B-Square.

"This might be an opportune time to leave, Mr. Jones," suggests one of his passengers.

"I agree," replies J. F. Jones.

Seeing the two hoodlums enter the freeway heading toward Ann Arbor, Jones decides to follow them as far as he can. On his cell phone, he calls the police to inform them of the crime just committed. He gives them the license-plate number, the description of the getaway car, and the direction they are headed. Then the passenger who had been doing all the talking up to this point picks up the conversation where he left off before stopping at the store.

"Nice job calling the police, Mr. Jones. So you mentioned having an acquaintance working at RNR Industries. What is his name, if you don't mind my asking?"

"His name is Benaiah Boyd, but we called him Ben. Do you know him?"

"That name sounds familiar. What about it, Bill?"

"Yeah, maybe so, David," replies the other man. "I know they have employed several gang members, and one gentleman goes by the name of Ben, who I understand has become an exceptional pilot, at least according to Eric Miller." After a few moments of silence from the limo driver and sensing his reference to Ben as a gang member might have struck a nerve with Mr. Jones, the man known as Bill continues the conversation. "So how do you know Ben?" he asks the limo driver.

"We were both in the same gang a few years ago," replies J. F. Jones.

"I'm sorry, Mr. Jones. I meant no disrespect. My name is Bill Rogers, and this is my colleague David Veil. We are from the Space Agency in Houston and have partnered with RNR Industries for several years now. Do you mind me asking what the name of your gang was called?"

Feeling a need to clear the air and let his passengers in on what he is doing, J. F. Jones tells them the gang was called B-Square in honor of their former leader, Benaiah Boyd. Mr. Jones goes on to tell them the two men who entered the coffee shop were wearing gang jackets with the B-Square insignia but insists his former gang had long since ceased their activities. As a lieutenant in the gang, Mr. Jones declares he knew every member in their organization and the two thugs who hit the coffee store are impostors. He ends by informing his passengers he was following them since they both were heading in the same direction in hopes of giving the police more information. He assures his passengers they are in no danger. Bill and David thank him for sharing his story and insist they are behind him in whatever decisions he would make.

Consistently exceeding the speed limit, both the limo and the dark, late-model Cadillac sedan they are following race past a state trooper sitting on a shoulder. J. F. Jones has time to slow his speed but instead accelerates, knowing the trooper would pursue. Within seconds, the state trooper is behind him but doesn't put on his beacon or siren. Instead, he flashes his high beams three times. David Veil looks out of the back window and states calmly that a highway-patrol car is following them. Bill Rogers comments that if he didn't know any better, he could swear the policeman just sent the Morse code for an SOS. The trooper continues to follow the limo as J. F. Jones follows the impostors, leaving enough space between them to not draw any attention. Likewise, the trooper is several car lengths behind the limo. The suspects slow to exit the freeway, and J. F. Jones tells his passengers he has a bad feeling in his gut. This is the same route he took earlier when he dropped off an elderly couple. The homes in this community are spaced hundreds of yards apart, so J. F. Jones pulls into a driveway several homes away from where the elderly couple lives. The state trooper likewise stops several yards behind him.

"My god, my god," whispers J. F. Jones audible enough for his passengers to hear him.

"What is it, Mr. Jones?" asks David Veil.

"Those imposters have just pulled into the home of the elderly couple," he says. "Please stay in the car," insists Mr. Jones.

J. F. Jones slowly exits his vehicle with his hands raised high over his head so that the approaching trooper can see him. "My name is J. F. Jones, Officer. I radioed in that the car I have been following was involved in a crime."

The trooper acknowledges he received a tip from his dispatcher concerning a dark, late-model Cadillac sedan suspected in a shooting just as the two vehicles raced by him. He suggests to J. F. Jones to wait by his vehicle as he investigates the scene. J. F.

Jones informs the trooper he happens to know an elderly couple living at the residence where the perpetrators have stopped. Waiting as instructed by the trooper, J. F. Jones watches as the officer cautiously approaches the home. The trooper pulls out his weapon and slowly enters the house. Suddenly, J. F. Jones hears two shots ring out. He thinks about rushing to the scene but decides against it. He then notices the two criminals rush out of the house and into their vehicle. J. F. Jones runs to the house, and to his surprise, the crooks ignore him as if they were on a mission. J. F. Jones enters the home and hears a woman screaming from an upstairs room. He rushes up the stairs to find the trooper lying facedown in the hallway. J. F. Jones identifies himself as he turns the officer over. The trooper is alive and informs the limo driver that backup is on its way and that he should check on the couple. J. F. Jones enters the room to find the elder woman weeping over her bleeding husband. Within minutes, a swarm of state and local police swarm the house. With them are David Veil, Bill Rogers, and emergency medical responders. The wounded officer insists to the paramedics to attend to the elderly gentleman. The wounded officer vouches for the limo driver. The elderly woman wants J. F. Jones to accompany her to the hospital, but he tells her he must drop off his passengers at a nearby research facility. Detectives on the scene allow J. F. Jones to transport his passengers to RNR Industries but also tell him they would like to meet him at the hospital for questioning.

4. How Can You Not Believe?

In the dark transport room now for over fifteen minutes, Dr. Erica Myers has an eerie feeling that someone is in the room with her. She shouts out, *"Is someone there? Hello? Can anyone hear me?"*

Seconds later, Erica hears a voice but cannot make out what the person is saying but is certain it is the voice of a male. As she continues to listen, he is speaking in a language that is not familiar to her. Somewhat frightened in this dark, unknown environment, she believes she could be dreaming or hallucinating and tries to calm herself by rubbing her hands over her arms. After several seconds, she once again hears someone speaking but again is unable to establish the person's dialect. Suddenly, one of her arms touches her vest pocket where she put the language translator Fashun Maddle gave her to test. Erica thinks to herself, *What the heck, it can't hurt!* She fumbles around with it for a few seconds, trying to get it activated while all the time hoping the voice she hears continues to speak. Suddenly, Erica hears the same dialogue the mysterious man in the room is speaking coming out of the translator. She then speaks out loud, "Come on, stupid thing. Translate to English." And to her surprise, the device responds, "Second language—English." Shocked and relieved at the same time, Erica quietly responds "Thank God!" Then unexpectedly, she hears the voice in the room reply, "Art thou a believer?"

Now Erica Myers is really scared as she realizes someone is indeed in the room. She then takes her first leap of faith and asks the person to walk toward her voice. Holding the translator with her left hand, she stretches out her right hand. Before it is fully extended, Erica feels a somewhat-rough hand touch hers, and she screams and retracts her hand.

The person calmly responds, "I am Philip. Who art thou?" Philip's strange dialect seems to have a soothing effect on Erica and comforts her.

She responds, "I am Dr. Erica Myers, but you can call me Erica."

"I have not heard of an angel whose name is Erica, nor would I believe the Lord need prepare a place for me in the presence of a doctor, seeing I am not sick. I must therefore assume this is not heaven," concludes Philip.

Erica chuckles at how extreme Philip's deduction of this room is but senses from his voice that he is sincere. She reaches out for Philip and, upon finding him, requests he sit down on the floor with her. "The ways you form your words are strange to me, Philip, but it could be this translator. This is definitely not heaven. Why would you think such a thing?" Erica asks.

"I thought my Lord had translated me," continues Philip. "I was concerned, however, that you found it difficult to communicate with me once I arrived here. You speak of a translator. Are you an angel of God with the power to translate his disciples?"

"Hold on, Philip," interrupts Erica. "I admit I do not read or know the Bible, but you talk like someone from biblical days. We are in an experimental room one of my colleagues built, and this room is on a spaceship. The translator I speak of allows people with different tongues to communicate with each other."

"Yet this translator of which you speak has brought me here?" infers Philip. "What is this Bible which you speak, and what sea is this vessel sailing on, may I ask, Angel Erica?"

"We are not on water or even on earth, Philip. We are above the earth in outer space," explains Erica. "In the heavens, so to speak. And have you no knowledge of the Bible?"

"So forgive me, Angel Erica, but first you say I'm not in heaven, yet now you admit we are above the earth, which is heaven? Is this a test? Are you not the same angel that sent me to the desert? And what is the Bible?"

Erica did not know who was more confused, her or Philip. "OK, Philip. All I know about the Bible is that it is a collection of scriptures men wrote a long time ago. But let us start over," insists Erica. "Where were you just before coming here? And what year was it?"

"Well, Angel Erica, I was witnessing to an Ethiopian eunuch in Gaza just outside Jerusalem," maintains Philip. "I am not sure of the year in which you speak. It has been over sixty years since the death and resurrection of our Lord, Jesus Christ, if that helps you."

"Oh my god, Philip. This can't be happening. What is going on here?"

"May I offer a suggestion, Angel Erica?" requests Philip.

"By all means, Philip, do so. And stop calling me an angel. I am so not that. Gee whiz, you got me talking like you now."

"Yes, Erica—an angel, I agree, thou most likely are not." Then Philip starts to give his explanation as to why he was here at this time. He tells Erica that an angel of the Lord spoke to him and told him to arise and go down from Jerusalem to Gaza where he found a man from Ethiopia sitting upon his chariot and reading from one of the prophets. The spirit of the Lord spoke to him to join himself to this man and his chariot. The man had a desire to worship, and he guided him through his reading, preaching unto him the crucified Jesus Christ and the baptism in his name. Seeing how the Lord sent him to a eunuch of great authority under Candace, the queen, he thinks it is therefore now possible that God has sent him to witness unto her.

"That is quite the explanation, Philip," declares Erica. "My friend, the guy who designed this room, is an elder in his church. One of the reasons we have not spoken or, shall I say, I have not communicated with him in months is due to something he told me concerning this salvation thing—for which, I admit, I know little about."

"This friend of yours will be rewarded for preaching unto you the gospel. No other duty unto man is more honorable than he that draws men unto Christ. Shall I continue, Erica?" asks Philip.

Erica thinks to herself how insane this whole thing is but is compelled to hear what Philip has to say. For a brief second, Erica ponders if this is some elaborate scheme concocted by Eric Miller to persuade her. Nevertheless, knowing she is trapped in this room, she replies, "Please continue, Philip!"

Outside the experimental room, George has been able to funnel enough energy for Canta and Albie with Eric Miller's guidance to activate the room's main console. Eric gives Albie a series of instructions to manually enter into the control panel and asks him to give him the results once he is finished. Within a few seconds, Albie finishes loading the commands into the system and waits for the calculated results. After a long minute, Albie replies to Eric that the number 62 has appeared on the panel, followed by an alternating message concerning the second occupant. All Albie and Canta can hear after that is Eric stating that this is not good.

"Hit the Escape button in the top left side of the control panel, Albie," commands Eric Miller.

"It says, 'Thirty minutes before system recharge completes,'" replies Albie.

"Now press the Menu button until you get to Room Status and then hit All," instructs Eric. "The room is sealed, and I need to know how much oxygen is in the room." After a few seconds, Eric hears the reply he feared from Albie.

"Less than thirty minutes," replies Albie. Muting his microphone, he grabs Canta's hand and tells her he doesn't believe Dr. Myers is going to make it.

Richard asks Dar to confirm the return of the anomaly appearing to be approaching the ship. Dar confirms, telling his navigational partner the same phenomenon they encountered earlier has indeed returned. Phair and Ion, overhearing the navigator's discussion, argue that their sensors are not picking up anything within a thousand kilometers of the cruise liner. However, Richard and Dar insist something is out there and heading their way. Fashun locates a pair of control gloves in a compartment on the commander's chair and puts them on. Extending her arms out shoulder-high, she uses her fingers to open a holographic projection of the exterior view of the ship. Moving her arms in a circular motion, she slowly visually surveys the exterior of the cruise liner and, in particular, the area Dar and Richard are referencing. The four students watch Fashun and her projection and wait patiently for her assessment. She finally concurs with Phair and Ion that nothing is out there. Richard explains how he modified the navigational arrays to sense temperature variations.

With the communications channel open, Benaiah Boyd listens to the conversation the young bridge crew is engaged in. He tells Eric Miller these kids might be on to something.

Benaiah asks Richard and Dar if they can record this incident and if they could determine if this phenomenon could be detected from a recording. Richard explains how they use temperature variations in space to detect this and Dar is working on an algorithm that should define the anomaly's shape. Eric Miller allows the young navigators to attend to Benaiah Boyd's request but does not want them to spend much time on it. He knows that if they are going to rescue Erica Myers, they will have to focus on engaging the hyperspace engines to produce enough residual energy to access the experimental room and free its occupants.

Eric Miller contacts General Westbrook and Professor Mueller, informing them of the situation with Dr. Myers and that the majority of the students are no longer on board the cruise liner. Eric tells General Westbrook about the strange phenomenon approaching the cruise liner, detected by the young bridge crew that remains on the ship. He asks if Bill Rogers and David Veil at the Space Agency could use their equipment to assist Richard, Dar, and Benaiah. General Westbrook informs Eric the Space Agency scientists have just arrived at RNR Industries and might be able to modify equipment on the premises to accommodate them. General Westbrook asks what this is all about, but Eric cannot give him any details.

Entering the conference room at RNR Industries, General Westbrook finds David Veil and Bill Rogers comforting Elizabeth Devereaux over the death of Helen Hayes. General Westbrook greets his colleagues and asks them about their trip, not realizing the drama they had experienced this night. Everyone gathers around the Space Agency scientists as they reminiscence about their ordeal. In all the excitement, David Veil does not realize he left his briefcase in the chauffeur's limousine. The faint sound of an incoming call to David Veil's satellite phone can be heard coming from the trunk of J. F. Jones's parked car.

J. F. Jones strolls into the emergency room at a college hospital and is immediately met by state-police investigators. His heart starts to pound as he reflects on his past when facing law-enforcement officials usually meant trouble. However, now that his life in gangs is behind him, he settles himself and walks up to the officers with confidence. Conversely, the police investigators have done their homework and know exactly who he is. Their questioning of the evening's events starts with J. F. Jones's call to the authorities on the store robbery. They theorize that he is actually part of the plot to rob the store and the elderly couple but something went horribly wrong. Keeping his composure, J. F. Jones tells them that if they truly believed that, he would have been taken into custody when he entered the hospital. He confirms his previously held position with the B-Square gang, followed by a summation of his verifiable actions the past few years. He then details what has transpired the past several hours. After jotting down some notes, the lead investigator urges J. F. Jones to stay in the area should they need to question him further. He gives J. F. Jones one of his business cards and requests that he calls if anything comes up and by no means should he take matters into his own hands. Before he leaves the ER, J. F. Jones asks one of the on-duty nurses the condition of the elderly GSW victim. One of them says he is still in surgery. He then asks if they had seen the victim's wife. The same nurse responds that she might be in the hospital chapel and gives him directions.

J. F. Jones walks slowly to the main floor's chapel, not knowing what other than his presence can be done or said to comfort the elderly woman whom he only met today. Opening the chapel doors, he spots her sitting quietly on the first pew. He quietly walks in and takes a seat on the second row behind her. Without looking back at him, she calls out his name and thanks him for coming.

"How, may I ask, did you know it was me?" asks J. F. Jones.

"Your cologne is rather distinct," she says. Turning around to face him, she lays her hand on his shoulder and confesses, "But I like it."

Dropping his head and using both his hands to sandwich her hand while removing it from his shoulder, he politely declares, "I don't even know your name."

"My name is Sharon Plummer, and my husband's name is Carl. But you can just call me Sharon."

"So how is Carl doing?" asks the chauffeur.

Sharon very calmly informs him that the surgery went well, they removed the bullet from his abdomen, and he is currently in recovery. Noticing how calm she is impresses J. F. Jones to the point he asks Sharon how it is she can be so calm and composed. Without hesitation, she replies that it is God who is strengthening her and is the one in complete control of this situation. Regardless of what happens to her husband, she is trusting in God completely. One way or another, God will give her understanding for this whole ordeal. She asks J. F. Jones if he is a Christian, but he drops his head, too ashamed to answer. Discerning this, Sharon comforts him by explaining it is never too late. Starting to cry, J. F. Jones utters that he wishes he could have done more to help them. Sharon, sandwiching both his hands with hers, stresses that he came back to check on them and is with her now and his being there is something neither she nor God will forget. Finally, J. F. Jones asks Sharon if she believes God will heal her husband. Sharon responds that God is in control and she trusts whatever he does, even if that means the death of her husband.

"If Carl dies, he will be in the presence of the Lord. And should he survive, he will continue to be with me. And if you knew Carl," Sharon says with a smile, "he would tell you the Lord is a tad bit better."

This kind of faith and trust in God is foreign to J. F. Jones, but he continues to listen as Sharon witnesses to him how God has performed many remarkable works in her life. J. F. Jones asks her how he could have this kind of faith. She explains that biblical faith only comes by hearing the word of God. She quotes the plan of salvation according to the scriptures and highlights Acts 2:38, which states that he needs to be baptized in Jesus's name and receive his Holy Spirit. The curious chauffeur replies that if God heals her husband, he might believe and do as she instructs.

Detective Purkins hangs up the phone on his desk and informs his partner, Detective Majours, that he is unable to reach David Veil. Sitting at a desk directly across from him, Detective Majours, looking through his notes, admits he does not have Bill Rogers's number. Detective Purkins admits he could not find it either and will have to wait for Mr. Veil to return his call. When Detective Majours asks if his partner left more than a request to return his call, Detective Purkins replies that he did not want to leave a voice message for David Veil informing him they are now classifying Helen Hayes's death as a homicide.

William Kennedy—having returned to Washington, DC—goes directly to his NIA office in nearby Virginia. In the hallway just outside his office, he receives through his satellite phone an incoming proximity-alert message from the spaceship under his control. Pressing a series of key commands, he pauses, waiting for an acknowledgment. Seconds later, the phone relays a response counting down from thirty seconds the self-destruction of the ship. He then opens a one-way audio channel to the cockpit of the ship, thanking the pilot, who is incapable of responding or resending the commands, for his blind loyalty. Entering his office and locking the door behind him, he calmly pulls out his chair and logs into a desktop computer, opening a secure connection to NORAD.

The lone engineer on-site at the tracking station notices one of the telescopes automatically repositioning to view the exact coordinates of the cruise liner. It is common for scientists with credentials to remotely access these systems, making adjustments for their researches. Standard operating procedures dictate the recording of events when such movements are detected.

William Kennedy is well aware of these procedures. This phase of his plan to discredit and portray the engineers at RNR Industries and the former B-Square gang members as terrorists is close to completion.

An audible voice emerges from the control panel outside the experimental transport room on the cruise liner. Albie Thayer inquires if Eric Miller was still listening and if he heard the same thing. Eric Miller quickly responds that he did and questions

George if the hyperspace engines are ready to go as life support in the room is down to sixty seconds. George replies the hyperdrive is fully online and can be activated. All residual energy will be routed to the transport room. Eric instructs Albie on George's signal to open the door to the room.

Richard Wright and Dar Skinner inform Fashun Maddle that the strange anomaly has once again reached the cruise liner. Fashun asks Eric and George for permission to execute the hyperdrive and warp speed on the course Richard and Dar have plotted. With his hand on a joystick-type throttle, Ion anxiously awaits Fashun's command. Ion hears Eric Miller give Fashun instructions to start a ten-second countdown. There is quiet on the bridge of the cruise liner as Fashun starts with "Ten." George is monitoring the residual-energy-flow indicators as he hears Fashun say nine and then eight. Albie takes hold of Canta's hand as he listens to Fashun deliberately count from seven to six.

On the asteroid Ceres, Eric Miller has his head bowed down and is quietly praying while Benaiah Boyd softly recites the twenty-third division of Psalm. Both men hear Fashun count from five to four.

On the bridge of the cruise liner, Richard and Dar have their eyes glued to Fashun as they hear her say three and then two. Phair Ghirl gives Ion a nod when she hears Fashun say one.

Suddenly, Fashun shouts out to Ion, "Execute, Einstein!"

Ion whispers just loud enough for Phair to hear him, "First name's Ion. Last name's Stein." Then with authority, he thrusts the handle all the way up.

In the control room at RNR Industries, one of the engineers sitting at his post notices a bright flash out of the corner of his eyes.

He scoots his chair over to the monitor where he believes the bright light came from, noticing it is the camera focused on the cruise liner. He does not notice the screen is dark until he types in a series of keystrokes to play back the last few frames. That is when he sees the tiny image of the cruise liner and then a bright light and the screen going dark. Puzzled at what just took place, he replays the same series of frames and enlarges the image. It is indeed the cruise liner, but then there is a blinding explosion causing the engineer to push back his chair in horror. *"She just blew up!"* he shouts. Running to the door of the control room, he shouts out louder, *"The cruise liner just blew up!"*

5. THE INNOCENT DIE

Staring at the telescope monitor, a scientist working alone at the NORAD tracking station is speechless after witnessing what appears to be an explosion. In the low-light control room filled with sophisticated telescopes and computer systems, red and amber lights flash, and warning messages scroll down various video screens. Having never experienced a situation like this, he temporarily ignores the alerts, rushing to find the emergency-protocol manual. Standing at the desk where the manual is located, he searches for and finds a list of procedures to follow. The first priority is to make sure all event recorders are online and operational. Still standing, he glances over his shoulder to the backup array of file servers and tape units, verifying the systems are recording by the movements of the tapes. Refocusing his attention on the protocol manual, he finds that the next step involves informing the NIA director, the only person requiring a personal, direct phone call. Taking a deep breath and walking away from the desk, he walks to a red phone programmed to connect to only one person.

NIA director William Kennedy pauses for a few seconds before answering the phone. Pretending to have no idea who is calling even though the caller ID displays "NORAD," Director Kennedy listens to the NORAD scientist before asking him if he recorded the event. The scientist is not sure if the director is testing him, so he quickly types in some commands and immediately responds that the uplink to the backup-storage server and the recording of the event are on their way to the director's terminal. NIA director William Kennedy checks his system for the feed and transfers it to his television monitor. Seeing the destruction for himself, he is now confident the only person capable of linking him to the tragedy at the Alpha Station has been eliminated. He is confident the public will be enraged with RNR Industries for not protecting the students. William Kennedy responds to the NORAD scientist, asking him for the coordinates of the explosion. When the young scientist responds, Director Kennedy implies that he believes an RNR Industries vessel with high school students on board was scheduled to be at those coordinates. He gives the scientist permission to give out whatever information he has to the public. Reluctant to respond, the scientist waits for further instructions only to hear a dial tone signifying the director's exit from the call.

The communications engineer at RNR Industries suspends and saves the current video recording showing what appears to be the complete destruction of the cruise liner and sends the feed to the adjacent main conference room. Most of the employees are in the conference room with David Veil and Bill Rogers and watching a local newscast covering the incident they were involved in. David and Bill tell everyone the limousine driver's instincts might just have saved the lives of the elderly couple. The two scientists from Houston dispute the report that an elderly man was killed. The hysterical and nearly out-of-breath engineer bursts into the conference room, heads straight for the video-conferencing system, and begs for everyone's attention for the screen. However, before he can start the feed, General Westbrook asks him to hold off as the news anchorman interrupts with news of a breaking story.

A news reporter says state-police investigators have not confirmed the identities of the assailants who fled the scene of the Ann Arbor community's home invasion, nor have they confirmed they were members of the gang once known as B-Square. Authorities do, however, believe the pair is responsible for at least one robbery at a coffee shop a few miles away from Detroit Metropolitan Airport. Police suspect robbery may have been the motive. The getaway vehicle is described as a dark, late-model Cadillac sedan. Authorities warn that if one sees this vehicle, they must not approach or otherwise provoke these men and call 911 immediately. Finally, tonight, the body of an unknown man was found in an alley of a Detroit neighborhood once ruled by the B-Square street gang. Details of his death as well as his identity have not yet been released. The anchorman pauses for a second as an assistant gives him several sheets of paper. "This just in," says the reporter. "Viewers from around the city have called in to the station regarding a bright light seen in the northern skies. The North American radar-tracking station known as NORAD has confirmed the light appears to be that of an explosion. A cruise liner owned and operated by RNR Industries was believed to be in the area of the suspected explosion. Our network crews are headed to Ann Arbor as we speak. All of this comes at the heels of another explosion that destroyed a deep-space outpost operated by a joint venture between RNR Industries and the Space Agency."

"What in the sam hill is going on?" shouts General Westbrook.

The control-room engineer blasts *"This is what I rushed in to show you!"* while using a remote control to switch the main viewing screen from television mode to video mode. *"I'm not sure how the news media got hold of this so quickly, but it appears as if the cruise liner just exploded."*

A view of the cruise liner appears on the screen, and suddenly, catching everyone by surprise, a bright explosion appears, followed by complete darkness. The shocked audience cannot believe what they have just seen. Some then start to cry, holding on to each other for support, while others declare this is just a hoax. Professor Mueller requests the feed be played back again, but the result is the same—the apparent total destruction of the cruise liner and its crew. After several minutes of utter silence, General Westbrook demands that the communications engineer contacts Eric Miller.

Eric Miller has lost his voice-communications link to the cruise liner, and Benaiah Boyd fears the worst. Eric believes the jump to hyperspace and the fact that the cruise liner's antenna array was not designed for long-range communications could be causing a temporary signal loss. Just when it seems as if Benaiah Boyd has regained his faith in God's protection of the cruise liner, Eric Miller receives an incoming message from RNR Industries. Benaiah's response is one of despair and shakes his head, suggesting bad news is about to come.

Having returned to the control room, the communications engineer repeats his message: "Eric Miller, this is the communications officer at RNR Industries. Do you read?"

"This is Eric Miller. Please continue," he replies.

In an attempt to appear unruffled and professional, the communications engineer informs Eric they have lost all audio and visual communications with the cruise liner and asks him to confirm. Eric calmly gives the communications officer the same rationale he gave Benaiah Boyd. With no immediate response from the communications engineer and sensing there is more, Eric looks at Benaiah, who is shaking his head in disbelief, and asks if there is any additional information the communications engineer would like to share. The communications officer states that one of their monitors picked up an explosion at the last-known coordinates of the cruise liner and requests Eric Miller to confirm. Overcome with grief, Benaiah Boyd grabs Eric Miller's shoulder before dropping to his knees. There is an eerie silence in Eric Miller's sunlit asteroid-belt laboratory. The communications engineer asks Eric Miller to acknowledge the receipt of his message for which Eric simply replies, "Acknowledged. We'll get back to you soon."

Eric extends his hand to his friend, Benaiah Boyd, and helps him to his feet. With a handheld computer, he insists to the former gang leader to walk with him to the flight deck. As they walk, Eric encourages Ben to keep the faith. Pointing his tablet computer at the *Argo Two*, Eric uploads the coordinates where the cruise liner should have materialized after its jump to hyperspace. Eric is fully confident the cruise liner's hyperdrive systems, being totally contained, would not create an explosion. Benaiah Boyd confesses he wishes he has faith like Eric's and prays there is a logical explanation for the explosion and that it is not at the expense of the cruise liner and its crew. However, he asks Eric to pray with him that God will increase his faith before Eric departs. The two servants of Christ pray aloud, crying out to God, and for the first time in months, Benaiah speaks in tongues as God's spirit is amplified in him. After several minutes of making their request known unto God, the two men embrace each other before

Benaiah, reaching into the back pocket of his bloody flight suit, retrieves the *Argo Two*'s control gloves, inserts his hands into them, and waves them at the ship, opening the *Argo Two* halo-doors and extending the entrance ramp. He enters the spacecraft and prepares to depart. Eric Miller, a deacon in his church and still whispering prayers, watches as the ramp quickly retracts and the halo-doors disappear into the shining black ship. Within seconds, the vessel slowly hovers and turns toward the bay doors. The noiseless engines are so balanced and quiet the only audible sound is that of the ship piercing the transparent decompression barrier, vanishing on a bluish trail of light.

J. F. Jones and Sharon Plummer have decided to leave the chapel and sit in a family waiting room until her husband comes out of recovery. Allowing Sharon to use his arm for balance, J. F. Jones continues to share his past, confessing his affiliation with the B-Square gang. Sharon patiently listens as her muscular friend escorts her to a vacant family waiting room. J. F. Jones makes Sharon comfortable on a lounger, and she asks him to turn off the television. Within a few seconds, she falls sound asleep. J. F. Jones locates a blanket, covers her, and turns off the lights. Having noticed a concession area a few yards from the waiting room, J. F. Jones leaves Sharon to see if there is coffee available. To his surprise upon entering the room, the emergency-room staff are gathered around a television monitor and watching the news. He locates a hot coffee pot full of the caffeinated beverage and, next to it, some Styrofoam cups. Having poured the mocha into the cup, he tastes it carefully as the steam from the cup indicates it is very hot. Placing a lid on the cup, he decides to join the assembly of duty nurses gathered around the television. They are so hypnotized by the broadcast they do not detect him in their presence.

"Recapping tonight's breaking story, a vessel believed to be operated by RNR Industries in a high earth orbit appears to have exploded, killing everyone on board. It has not been confirmed, but sources close to RNR Industries tell our newsroom there could have been as many as fifty Michigan high school students on board the ship. RNR Industries has been in the news as of late concerning another deep-space explosion of the Alpha Station, where two civilian scientists were presumed killed. As many of our viewers are aware, RNR Industries is at the center of controversy concerning its relationship with former gang members turned astronauts. And this just in to our newsroom: Reporters are on the scene of a homicide at a west-side strip club. Witnesses say two men wearing B-Square jackets entered the My Girl gentleman's club and asked the bartender for the establishment's owner. When Mr. Haywood Hughes came out, the assailants asked if he was Mr. Hughes, apparently not recognizing him by face. Witnesses say the pair pulled out automatic weapons and opened fire on Mr. Hughes, killing him instantly. All witnesses were consistent in their accounts that the suspects shouted 'That's from King Dog' before fleeing the scene in a dark-colored Cadillac sedan. No other persons were injured. It is believed 'King Dog' is in reference to purported B-Square enforcer Killin 'King Dog' Daly. Daly was released earlier this year after spending the past ten years in the state penitentiary for second-degree murder in the beating death of a rival gang kingpin. It was the testimony of Hughes that led to Killin Daly's conviction—the only B-Square member ever convicted and sentenced of a crime. Please stay tuned to this station for updates as they occur."

Immediately following the end of this television story, J. F. Jones pocket phone rings. The caller is his wife and partner since high school, inquiring his whereabouts. Having heard the same news reports, she is concerned for his safety. She goes on to describe a strange vehicle parked in front of their home. She says their daughter saw two men exit a dark-colored Cadillac and get into a late-model BMW. J. F. Jones begs her to stay vigilant inside their home until he arrives. He is already aware that the vehicle in front of their home matches the description of the car reported speeding away from the night club. Not wanting to alarm her, the car she described likewise matches the description of the vehicle he and police have been tracking all night. Before ending the call, he suggests she arms herself. She acknowledges his request by informing him she has been holding a loaded pistol during their entire conversation.

Hastening back to the waiting room, J. F. Jones finds Sharon wide awake and talking to a nurse. Upon entering the room, a jubilant Sharon Plummer turns her attention to J. F. Jones. "They have transferred Carl to a private room," declares Sharon. She looks back at the nurse and proclaims that the gentleman entering the room will accompany her to her husband's room, stretching forth her arm toward J. F. Jones and posturing herself for him to assist her.

At the moment J. F. Jones's hands touch Sharon's to help her to her feet, he senses a strange presence come over him. Sharon continues to repeat her husband's room number while they walk down the hallway, sensing the chauffeur is preoccupied with something else. Finally, she asks J. F. Jones what is bothering him. He explains the situation at his home to her as they enter her husband's room. After he escorts Sharon to her husband's bedside, she touches her husband's left arm lying outside the sheets, and he opens his eyes. Speaking ever so softly, Sharon leans down to hear what he has to say. Within seconds, she laughs and kisses him on the head while he closes his eyes to rest.

"What is it?" asks J. F. Jones.

"Carl wanted to know why I was hanging out with a younger guy instead of being by his side."

Sharon thanks J. F. Jones for assisting her and encourages him to hasten to his family. They embrace each other, and J. F. Jones moves toward the door and stops.

"What's on your mind, young man?" asks Sharon.

"I have seen the working of your god, for he has destroyed my disbelief! I must get this baptism and the Holy Spirit," he demands.

"Come back to us when you have settled your family," she replies. "There is a church on Packard Road here in town. They will baptize you, my friend. Now go attend to your family."

Acknowledging her words by nodding his head, J. F. Jones rushes from the room and exits the hospital. Spotting his parked limousine, the chauffeur retrieves the state-police investigator's card from his vest pocket. He considers calling the detective but fears law-enforcement agents would arrive at his home prior to his arrival and would confront his wife, which might not end well.

Outside a Houston funeral home, Miriam Hayes greets neighbors and friends who are departing after a memorial service held for her sister Helen. A woman extends her hand to Miriam Hayes and introduces herself as the wife of David Veil. She says her husband was a colleague of Ms. Hayes, but due to a business trip, he and several other close associates from the Space Agency are unable to attend. Miriam Hayes smiles and thanks her for coming. Continuing down the sidewalk, Mrs. Veil is stopped by two men she assumed were also at the funeral home to pay their final respects to the memory of Helen Hayes.

"Hello, Mrs. Veil. Is that correct?" asks one of the men.

"Yes, that's right. I'm Mrs. Veil," she reluctantly replies.

"My name is Detectives Purkins," he announces, holding his badge in one hand and using his other hand to point to the other man. "And this is my partner, Detective Majours. We are the chief investigators in Helen Hayes's death."

A surprised Mrs. Veil looks at Detective Purkins and responds, "I thought Helen's death was an accident! What is there to investigate?"

Addressing Mrs. Veil's question in a manner not to be heard by anyone else, Detective Purkins replies, "We thought so too, Mrs. Veil, but the medical examiner's office came up with data we wanted to share with your husband. Unfortunately, our repeated efforts to reach him have been unsuccessful." Having waited a few seconds without receiving a reaction from Mrs. Veil, Detective Purkins continues, "The next time you speak to him, please have him contact us immediately."

Mrs. Veil acknowledges the two detectives and walks away. She is careful not to give them any further reason to be concerned, but she too has become curious as to why her husband has not contacted her upon his assumed safe arrival in Detroit.

At RNR Industries, Professor Mueller, at General Westbrook's request, has arranged for a coach line bus to meet Grace Gryer at Eric Miller's home. He has ordered her to bring all the students back to the campus of RNR Industries and demands they do not contact anyone. She is to instruct the coach driver to use a private drive behind the runways leading to the hangars to avoid the media camped out at the front gate. Believing Sarah Davies is well enough to travel, he likewise insists to Grace to bring Sarah and her husband, William, along as well. News crews have assembled themselves at the main gate at RNR Industries like flies on poop. To divert their attention from the rear of the campus, General Westbrook has sent them a message that he is prepared to make a statement. Grace Gryer will call Professor Mueller when she is outside the locked gate. Professor Mueller will then relay that message to General Westbrook who will give a statement to reporters anxious to grab headlines.

Police normally patrol the neighborhood of Judge Wright, but this evening, the judge notices an unusual amount of activity with patrol cars stopping for minutes at a time in front of his home. Knowing his son was on board the apparently destroyed cruise liner, he fears reporters will not cease to get his opinion and feed on his family's tragic loss. Explaining this to his wife, Judge Wright asks her to pack up some clothes as they will be spending some time in Ann Arbor. He wants to be as close to RNR Industries as he can when reports of his son's demise are confirmed.

Approaching his home in the Detroit suburb of Inkster, J. F. Jones spots a Cadillac parked in front of his home. He slowly pulls into his driveway and confirms from the license plate it is indeed the vehicle he and police have been following. Before he exits his limousine sedan, he briefly surveys the street to make sure police are not in the area and waiting to do something stupid. He calls his wife, confirming she is safe, and lets her know he is at home and preparing to enter their house. Upon walking in the front door, he notices his wife still holding firm her revolver. He begs her to lower and table the weapon before giving her a big, long hug. His daughter, recognizing his presence in the home, approaches her parents and joins in the extended group hug. Confident they are safe and alone, J. F. Jones retrieves the phone number from the card the detective gave him, rings the investigator's number, and alerts him to the location of his residence and the abandoned vehicle they have been searching for parked in front of it. He also makes it clear he and his wife and daughter are inside their home and have absolutely nothing to do with this. He asks if the state trooper who assisted him at the Ann Arbor shooting could join the officers who undoubtedly would be paying him a visit. Within minutes, his house is swarmed with police from several agencies. Having invited them into his home, J. F. Jones is not prepared to make a statement until the investigator and state trooper from the crime scene and hospital arrived. Approximately ten long minutes later, the two law-enforcement agents arrive and confirm J. F. Jones's innocence. At which time, he has his daughter explain the time the Cadillac appeared and the BMW that rescued its occupants. Crime-scene investigators have finished scrubbing down the Cadillac and are preparing to tow it away. During the investigator's interview, one of the officers' radios reports a BMW matching the description given by Jones's daughter was spotted in the neighborhood of Judge Wright's home.

At RNR Industries, a rather-sizable contingency of news reporters and camera crews have assembled at the guarded gate leading to the campus offices. General Westbrook is at the front door of the main office building just yards away from the guarded gate. Professor Mueller, still in the conference room, receives a call from Grace Gryer informing him the charter bus is at the security gate on the opposite side of the campus. She is about to disembark and enter the security code to open the gate. Professor Mueller ends the call and immediately walks to the building entrance where General Westbrook is waiting. Without speaking a word, Professor Mueller nods his head, signaling the time has arrived for them to address the reporters. General Westbrook has commanded everyone with the exception of Professor Mueller to stay inside and out of camera sight. He and Professor Mueller walk out to meet them. The guards, aware of the plan, open the gates and are immediately rushed by reporters and their camera crews.

The first to reach General Westbrook is a female reporter who immediately asks, "General Westbrook, what can you tell us about the destruction of the Alpha Station and the scientists who were assigned there?"

"Right now, young lady, all I'm prepared to say is that our internal investigation is still ongoing and we are presently reviewing data. There is no concrete evidence supporting the loss of the station or its occupants."

A young male reporter shouts out, "Isn't it true this facility sent a spaceship to the Alpha Station at the same time of the alleged explosion?"

Professor Mueller calmly responds, "RNR Industries indeed has a deep-space ship that was scheduled to enter the same region of space as the Alpha Station. We have temporarily lost communications with the ship and its pilot but have no reason to believe the ship or the pilot made contact with the station or its custodians. We will be able to make a more definitive statement once we have reviewed all our data and reestablished communications with the ship."

The same reporter is quick to ask another question. "Is it also true that the pilot of that ship is also a member of the B-Square street gang?"

"Former member," passionately interjects Professor Mueller.

A third middle-aged male reporter, directing his question to Professor Mueller, asks, "Are you aware that members of the B-Square street gang, whom you have been training, have been seen committing acts of terror today all across this region?"

"That is news to us," surprisingly responds General Westbrook. "I'm afraid this will have to end our interview. Thank you all for coming and being patient with us."

Professor Mueller and General Westbrook quickly retreat back into the solitude of RNR Industries. Once inside, they discover most of the staff gathered around a television monitor, having just watched the live telecast of their media interview.

"Once again, a recap of today's top story: Police agencies across Southeastern Michigan are asking the public for any information leading to the apprehension of at least two members of the B-Square street gang. The pair and possibly others are wanted in connection with violent crimes across multiple counties, the most recent one at a Detroit club and resulting in the death of the club's owner. Investigators are puzzled by the recent attacks as it was thought the B-Square organization was reformed and had departed from any criminal activities. They have reportedly been involved with technological programs at an Ann Arbor–based aerospace-manufacturing company. The former leader of the gang could not be reached for comment, but his first lieutenant, who did not wish to appear on camera, stated just hours ago after the last attack that his transformed organization is not involved with these recent acts of violence."

6. Our Leaders Lie

The staff at RNR Industries welcome Professor Mueller and General Westbrook back from their brief interview with local reporters. The communications engineer, standing a few yards away from General Westbrook and Professor Mueller, asks a question that causes everyone present to stop talking, waiting for a response. "General Westbrook, did you and Professor Mueller just lie to reporters?" he asks.

"We omitted some facts, son, and in my book, that is not a lie!" replies General Westbrook with a straight face.

William Kennedy prepares for a news briefing but continues to keep a watchful eye on the NORAD monitors as if to capture a glimpse of anything that would lead him to believe either the cruise liner or his cloaked ship was not totally destroyed. It takes him roughly twenty minutes to complete his speech to the press. During this time, he is now confident the cloaked ship he destroyed was successful in taking out the cruise liner also. There are no signs of life from that sector of space or any moving trajectories that could resemble the presence of a spacecraft, so William Kennedy shuts down the monitors. Confident his message to the press will add more public suspicion and outrage to the operations of RNR

Industries, he outputs the pages to his local printer. Brandishing his sports coat around and making sure it has not even a spot of lint before slipping it on and inserting his carefully worded speech into his inner pocket, the NIA director checks himself in a mirror behind his closed door one more time before arrogantly leaving his office.

Approaching the entrance of the original headquarters building (OHB) on his way to an auditorium, William Kennedy is met by a small contingent of reporters. He realizes the journalists waiting to question him in the room known as the Bubble will have sophisticated audiovisual equipment capable of relaying his message to the world, and he does not want to divulge such thrilling information prematurely to columnists looking for a quick story. So without saying a word, William Kennedy points to a stone wall, and then he states the inscription written on it. "Ye shall know the truth, and the truth shall make you free." With an egotistical smile on his face, William Kennedy arrogantly exits the OHB.

All the major television networks have preempted their normal broadcasts to bring the news of the accident in space, unaware that the story was leaked from this very office. Among the audiences tuning in to this newscast are the entire staff at RNR Industries, the employees at the Space Agency, the police investigators in Ann Arbor, and J. F. Jones and his family.

Swiftly entering the auditorium known as the Bubble, William Kennedy walks directly to the podium and, without hesitation, begins his press conference. "Let me ask that you hold your questions until I signal that you may ask them. It is with tremendous sorrow that I report the destruction of a civilian-operated, space-orbiting cruise liner. Even more horrendous is the fact that the majority of its passengers were high school scholars.

This agency believes a vicious, cold-blooded act of terrorism was carried out by a terrorist group headquartered in Detroit known as B-Square. Several of its members including its felonious leader, operating under the pretense of reformed hoodlums, infiltrated the ranks of RNR Industries. While we believe RNR Industries was not directly responsible for the attack, they did nothing to screen these terrorists for the prevention of such a tragic and senseless loss of life. Details of the attack cannot be revealed as the data is currently under review. I'd also like to comment on a story you have been reporting concerning a deep-space facility known as the Alpha Station. This office has evidence that the former leader of this B-Square street gang is responsible for its destruction and the deaths of two civilian scientists on board. It is believed his inexperience in interstellar piloting cost him his life as well. But let it be known that criminal charges against the surviving menaces to society are being prepared and justice will be swift and stern. Because of the lack of leadership at the Space Agency—particularly from General Westbrook, who has been working with RNR Industries—this office is pursuing the immediate takeover of all Space Agency activities and seeking an injunction to cease all activities at RNR Industries."

The reporters at William Kennedy's press conference, shouting all at once, begin to question how this gang could be able to pull off such a monumental feat and what their motives were for doing so.

Professor Mueller mumbles to those in attendance at RNR Industries, "This should be good!"

William Kennedy, waving his stretched-out hands up and down to settle the crowd of reporters, continues by telling them the NIA has been monitoring activities at RNR Industries, believing they are responsible for the death of the former NIA director, who happened to be his brother. William Kennedy tells a now-quiet and attentive audience seeking a motive that RNR Industries, in conjunction with members of the Space Agency, have been hoarding knowledge involving a region of space that has regenerative powers. Approximately two years ago, a mission to the constellation Cygnus revealed that a virtual fountain of youth exists by traveling at greater-than-light speeds through that sector of space. When William Kennedy's brother discovered this secret, his spacecraft was sabotaged, killing him and his crew just after takeoff. Subsequently, a monitoring station known as the Alpha Station was established to make certain no other agencies outside the Space Agency or organizations outside RNR Industries would gain access to this power. As the NIA moved closer to exposing the truth, a rogue element within RNR Industries, known to the world as the B-Square street gang, was brought on board as enforcers. "This gang appears to have taken advantage of the training RNR Industries afforded them to establish a new agenda. As I stated earlier, the leader of this gang used an RNR Industries vessel to destroy the Alpha Station and murder the station's facilitators."

The flock of reporters erupts with questions relative to the motives a street gang and the Space Agency would have for stealing information owned by RNR Industries even if they were already partners. They also vehemently question why RNR Industries would use a gang it was publicly attempting to reform to murder and seize control over technology they already owned. Other reporters shout to have the NIA director address the reasons RNR Industries would have for killing innocent children they were attempting to assist.

Once again waving his arms up and down and soliciting the audience's silence while remaining calm as if he planted the questions among selected reporters, William Kennedy uses the last comments he heard concerning the apparent death of the children to his advantage. Thanking them for bringing that issue back up as he wants to expound on it, he explains to the journalists that his staff at the NIA was likewise perplexed as to why RNR Industries would assault their own personnel. However, they were able to ascertain that one of the chief scientists, a supposed Christian named Eric Miller, and the leader of the gang, Benaiah Boyd, are using fear and intimidation to gain exclusive control of this technology for their own selfish, power-hungry agenda. He begs the media correspondents to remember it is an RNR vessel believed to be piloted by Benaiah Boyd that destroyed the Alpha Station the week before. "I'll take one more question," he says.

A reporter in the front row asks, "Can you comment on the recent rash of violence inflicted by the B-Square gang in and around the Detroit metropolitan area?"

"More proof these lunatics are out of control," concludes NIA director Walter Kennedy.

However, as he begins to exit the podium, a reporter catches him off guard by soliciting comments regarding him avenging his brother's death by attacking RNR Industries.

Stopping dead in his tracks and pausing for several seconds before slowly returning to the podium, a visibly shaken William Kennedy responds. "Let me be perfectly clear. These cold, indiscriminate barbarians killed my brother. If you or anyone else thinks differently, you are morons! Furthermore, if you think I would use this forum, the deaths of innocent scientists and children, as a means for revenge, you are as misguided and egotistical as those responsible for my brother's demise."

With that statement, the newsmen quietly paused to reflect on William Kennedy's statement, watching him passionately storm off the lectern. Once in the seclusion of the hallway, he regains his composure, wondering whether the journalist is actually going to allow him to exit the stage as he was the only person pain to have that very question asked. But now seeds of doubt and mistrust have been firmly planted and watered in the public's mind concerning RNR Industries, their relationship with the B-Square gang, and the death of his brother.

The employees at RNR Industries watching this telecast are infuriated by William Kennedy's accusations against the former gang, knowing the caliber of the men they have trained. They are equally incensed by his indictment against them concerning the death of his brother. David Veil and Bill Rodgers walk over to Professor Mueller and inform him he has their complete cooperation and do not for a moment believe anything William Kennedy has said concerning the integrity and motives of RNR Industries. General Westbrook, standing next to Professor Mueller, in like fashion gave him his support but warned the burden of proof has now shifted to this team and that he was still in control of the Space Agency at the moment and will do everything in his power to disclaim these outrageous allegations and vindicate their companions. He suggests, however, their primary concern now is to determine the exact nature of the explosion and the fate of their comrades.

General Westbrook, looking among the sober crowd in the conference room, attracts the attention of Professor Mueller who asks, "What or who are you looking for, General?"

"I'm looking for that communications engineer," calmly replies General Westbrook. "He has got to be the only person not watching the news. I want him to get back in touch with Eric Miller. I need to know the status of his plan and whether or not it is successful."

Then to everyone's surprise, the communications engineer rushes into the room while doing what is fast becoming a trademark of his—shouting for Grace Gryer. Professor Mueller shouts out that Grace is most likely with the students and curiously inquires why he is looking for Grace.

The excited communications engineer fights his way over to where Professor Mueller, General Westbrook, David Veil, and Bill Rogers are huddled. "Grace is always repeating a Bible scripture that says 'Hope that is seen is not hope.' Those words of hope kept ringing in my head, so I decided to exercise my hope and look for something I cannot see." The motivated communications engineer once again switches the video screen from television mode to play back the scene from the cruise liner's explosion. The communications engineer points to an area on the screen. To the naked eye, no one in the room can see anything but a massive explosion.

"What are we supposed to be looking at?" asks a rather-impatient General Westbrook.

The communications engineer rewinds the video feed and forwards it in slow motion, asking the team to focus on a section slightly away from the main blast. Watching the elapsing time counter, he stops the video and asks them to take a close look at what follows. Advancing the video one frame at a time, there appears to be another flash in concert with the main explosion, lasting only a millisecond. He plays it again at regular speed, and nothing appears, but then frame by frame he points to an ever-so-small flash just before the massive explosion.

"That means nothing, son," explains General Westbrook. "An explosion of this magnitude could have resulted in several smaller ones."

"Play that back a frame at a time," asks Bill Rodgers. "I think he might have something, General Westbrook. This flash is well defined and takes place just before the main explosion, which indicates it is not part of the explosion." Bill Rogers asks the communications engineer to repeat just the frames in question. Upon further examination, the veteran space-administration scientist determines the flash appears to be in the form of a straight line and vanishes too quickly to be extinguished even in the vacuum of space.

"I still don't follow you, Bill," admits General Westbrook. "What do you think it means?"

At this time, everyone in the conference room has seen the video and heard the ensuing conversation. Elizabeth Devereaux walks over to General Westbrook and, wrapping her arms around him, responds, "It means we have hope, General."

The *Argo Two*, piloted by Benaiah Boyd, enters the parsec of space where the cruise liner should have appeared according to the navigational trajectory supplied by Eric Miller. Engaging his short-range sensors, he opens up a communications link to Eric Miller on the Ceres Asteroid. "Eric, this is the *Argo Two*. Do you read?"

"I read you, *Argo Two*. What's going on?" calmly asks Eric Miller.

"I have nothing on short-range scanners. Switching over to long-range now." After pausing for a few seconds, Benaiah Boyd continues. "The only things I have on long-range scanners are earth and its moon. I'm dropping out of hyperspace and proceeding at one-quarter light. I'll be approaching the dark side of the moon and trying to stay hidden from earth's tracking systems."

"Excellent move, Ben," replies Eric. "The sensors are more sensitive at sublight speeds. Keep this channel open, and try hailing the cruise liner. You might want to open the forward viewer to get a visual."

The sudden jump to hyperspace followed by a sudden stop has shut down the engines on the cruise liner and rendered the crew unconscious. After several attempts to contact someone, Benaiah Boyd's message is finally heard by Fashun Maddle, who gradually comes to her senses. Noticing she is the first to regain consciousness, Fashun Maddle instinctively rushes to the aid of Ion Stein, shaking and yelling for him to wake up. As Ion Stein starts to regain consciousness, Fashun traverses the bridge, verifying each of the other members of her junior bridge crew is conscious and coherent. Returning to the captain's chair, she instructs her team to give her a status check according to each of their positions. She locates the communications section on the arm of the chair and figures out how to open a ship-wide channel. She asks if George Lee in engineering is conscious enough to let her know and give a status on the engines. Likewise, she asks Albie Thayer to report on his condition and that of Canta Cee's.

The first to report in is Ion. "I do not have helm control, Fashun," he calmly states. "We are on emergency power and appear to be several thousand miles above the moon's surface in a steady descent."

"Copy that, Helm," replies Richard Wright from his navigation console. "The ship is in a slow yet continuous descent to the surface." He opens the forward viewing screen, but everything is totally black.

Fashun remarks that she can't see the moon or the stars. Dar Skinner then replies it is because they are on the dark side of the moon.

Realizing the *Argo Two* is waiting for her response, Fashun Maddle attempts to acknowledge the hail, but the channel is not responsive.

George Lee in engineering, having heard everything that has transpired, hails the bridge. "Fashun, this is George Lee in engineering. The engines are off-line, and without Eric Miller's assistance, I am afraid I can do nothing. I do know, however, that RNR Industries–manufactured vessels have their own short-range ship-to-ship-communications systems in cases of emergencies. If you are receiving a hail from the *Argo Two*, it is probably because he is using the emergency-communications systems and is in relatively close proximity to us."

"How do I activate this system?" asks Fashun.

"You cannot, Fashun," answers George as Fashun drops her head in despair. "You are not authorized to do so, but I can." Still wearing a pair of control gloves, George activates a holographic-communications console. He adds the *Argo Two* and *Argo Navis* to the ship-to-ship-communications link.

"*Argo Two*, this is George Lee on the cruise liner, over."

Immediately Benaiah Boyd responds, "Glory be to God, George. I hear you loud and clear. Where in the world are you?" he asks.

But before gathering any more data from George Lee, Benaiah, reestablishing his communications link with Eric Miller, says, "I got them, Eric. Glory be to God. I've got them. I'm still unable to locate them on scanners, but I got them."

On the Ceres Asteroid, Eric Miller raises his arms to heaven, praying out loud to God and thanking him for blessing this young crew. He wipes a tear from his eye and responds. "I'm going to the *Argo Navis*, Ben, and enabling the communications systems. Please add the *Argo Navis* to your ship-to-ship-communications link."

While waiting for the *Argo Two* to reopen communications, George contacts Albie Thayer for a status update on the experimental room. Canta Cee, having received information from Albie, explains that power and life support have been restored to the chamber occupied by Dr. Erica Myers, but the doors cannot be open. All other systems appear to have been reset by the maneuver. George asks Albie to lead Canta to engineering where she will be of use should Eric need her expertise. George Lee returns to the bridge concurrently with the *Argo Two* establishing communications.

"Cruise Liner, this is Benaiah Boyd on board the *Argo Two*. Do you read?"

"We copy, *Argo Two*. This is George Lee on the bridge of the cruise liner."

"Sorry for interrupting our conversation, George, but I want to bring in Eric Miller. *Argo Navis*, do you read us?"

"Yes, *Argo Two*. This is Eric Miller on board the *Argo Navis*. I read you both. Good to hear your voice again, G. How is Dr. Myers? Were you able to extract her from the room?" inquires Eric.

"Likewise, Eric. Good to hear your voice one more time," insists George. "Power was restored to the chamber, and conditions reset. However, the door to the room will not open. Any suggestions?"

"I have not left the hangar bay on Ceres. I should be able to transport Dr. Myers to the room here in my lab. Stand by."

Eric Miller quickly leaves the bridge of the *Argo Navis*, literally sliding down the ramp and onto the floor of the hangar bay. Running to the control room on the asteroid, he quickly establishes a link to the room on the cruise liner. Working the controls as if they are musical instruments, he transports a single being from the chamber on the cruise liner to the chamber on the asteroid, praying it is the woman he has come to realize he is in love with. The display on the control panel reads "Transport sequence complete," and the door of the experimental room opens. Breaking the plane of the door, a light comes on in the room, exposing a woman lying on the floor. Deep within his spirit, he believes she is alive. He quickly walks and kneels down behind her and places his left hand on her head and checks with his right hand her right hand for a pulse and then softly whispers in her ear, "Ricky, this is Eric. Are you all right?"

An eternal second passes before she rolls toward him and calmly replies, "I like it when you call me that. Now if you are real, hold me tight so I can feel you!"

Eric Miller wraps both his arms around Erica Myers and squeezes her tight. With tears in both their eyes, Eric kisses Erica for the first time on her cheek. Helping her to her feet, he states that that is something he has wanted to do since elementary school. Wiping the water from his eyes, he welcomes Dr. Erica Myers to the Ceres Asteroid. "We have a lot of catching up to do, Dr. Myers," explains Eric Miller. "I have been communicating with the cruise liner through the *Argo Navis*'s ship-to-ship-communications systems. Before we return to the hangar bay, I need to contact RNR Industries. Make yourself at home, Erica."

Walking around the open floor plan on Eric Miller's asteroid laboratory, Erica Myers ponders in her heart if Eric came here to put some distance between the two of them.

"RNR Industries, this is Eric Miller on the Ceres Asteroid. Do your read?" Eric waits sixty seconds or so before repeating his hail. After the third time, he receives a reply from the communications engineer.

"This is the communications engineer, Eric Miller. We have been waiting to hear from you. Present with me is General Westbrook, Professor Mueller, David Veil, and Bill Rogers. Have you been able to ascertain any information on the cruise liner and the condition of Dr. Myers?"

Motioning for Erica Myers to come near, Eric signals for her to give them a response.

"Hello, everyone. This is Dr. Erica Myers. I'm on the asteroid with my old friend, Eric Miller, and doing fine. I'm not sure about my colleagues on the cruise liner."

An overjoyed General Westbrook interjects, "Dr. Myers, I can't tell you how relieved I am to hear your voice."

However, everyone at RNR Industries begins to sense that maybe Dr. Myers is the only survivor of the ill-fated cruise liner. General Westbrook nervously continues, "What is the status of your crew?"

Eric Miller interjects that the crew is still alive, but the only way to communicate with them is with the secure ship-to-ship-communications systems as the interstellar-communications array on the cruise liner is damaged. He and Dr. Myers will be going on board the *Argo Navis* to assess their condition. They will update RNR Industries within the hour from the *Argo Navis*. Eric requests the team there to prepare for the arrival of all ships back to earth.

Eric Miller starts a shutdown subroutine for nonessential systems on the asteroid. Extending his arm toward Erica Myers, she takes hold of him with both her hands as her full strength has not yet returned. Once on board the *Argo Navis*, Erica Myers acknowledges how good it feels to be back on board the ship that brought her, Eric, and George together. She naturally assumes her position at the navigation console as Eric Miller reconnects with the cruise liner and *Argo Two*.

Looking in Erica's direction and smiling, Eric Miller concludes, "George, I have our running buddy, Dr. Myers, with me. We are preparing to leave Ceres. Have you ascertained the position and condition of your ship?"

"Yes, Eric," acknowledges George. "Fashun Maddle has done an exemplary job of assessing our condition and position. I am delighted to hear Erica is safe. She is, without a doubt, in good hands. However, the news regarding our position is not good."

"Please clarify," inquires Eric.

George explains that he and his freshman crew have come to the conclusion that the power needed to generate enough residual energy to bring the experimental room back online caused the engines to lock up. Emergency protocols shut the engines down before the ship could continue on its intended course. As a result, they are several thousand miles above the dark side of the moon's surface and in a slow but rapidly increasingly descent. Dar Skinner estimates they will crash in less than an hour. Canta is currently in engineering but does not know how to restart the engines. George enlists Eric's knowledge of the engines to assist her.

All along, Erica Myers has established communications with RNR Industries. Even while not wanting to interrupt until George finished his assessment of the situation, David Veil chimes in that he and the staff in Ann Arbor have heard George's evaluation and stand ready to assist.

Eric Miller knows the engines can be restarted but not in time to prevent the crash landing of the cruise liner. Erica informs Eric that she has plotted a course to the moon and is ready when he is. Erica Myers begs Eric to turn the ship over to navigational control. She will have them clear of the rocks in twenty seconds and ready for the jump to hyperspace.

Dr. Myers asks Eric if he trusts her. He jokingly responds that that is an unusual question to ask him with Benaiah Boyd, George, and the entire crew of the cruise liner and certain select members of RNR Industries all listening. Nevertheless, he replies that he trusts her with his life and hopes that whatever she is up to does not require that sort of a sacrifice. She explains she might have a plan to save the cruise liner but will need the assistance of David Veil and Bill Rogers to validate her theory.

"I'm all ears, Doc!" subscribes Eric.

Dr. Myers believes that if the *Argo Two*, traveling at hyperspeed, could pass close enough to the cruise liner between it and the moon, the resulting wake would be able to alter the cruise liner's trajectory, pushing it out of the moon's gravitational pull. Benaiah Boyd responds he is ready and asks them to just send him the plotted course, but Eric, looking at Erica, shakes his head from side to side, indicating that it is probably not a good idea. Bill Rogers thinks it might work but said he would need to enter some variables into a computer simulation of this scenario. He does not have his pocket computer and asks David Veil to borrow his. David believes his computer is with his briefcase, and both are in the conference room but do not recall having them since leaving the airport. The communications engineer logs into a computer in the control room and suggests to Bill to tunnel into one of the Space Agency's systems. All is quiet on all three ships and in the control room as Bill Rogers creates a simulation. Turning back to the others, Bill says the *Argo Two* is just too small to affect the cruise liner's descent. Dr. Myers then asks Bill to enter the weight of the *Argo Navis*, a much-larger ship, in his simulation. Once again, quietly anticipating a positive response rests on everyone's minds. Without turning around, Bill whispers it might work. Professor Mueller walks over to the computer where Bill Rogers is still feverously typing in commands, verifies Bill has a working scenario, and informs his colleagues at RNR Industries of the same. Bill rushes back to the communications console, explaining to Dr. Myers what she will need to do. George relays the coordinates of the cruise liner to Dr. Myers, and she enters them along with a course correction into the *Argo Navis's* navigational computers. She then instructs George that he will have to manually pilot the cruise liner as it is unpredictable where or what direction his vessel will be pointing at as a result of the wake. Eric Miller suggests they all strap in as the cruise liner's stabilizers will probably not be too effective. Erica Myers signals to Eric that she is ready for him to engage. Eric warns George that the data given him by Erica puts them on the scene in less than fifteen minutes and that Ben should move the *Argo Two* well away from the moon. While engaging the

Argo Navis's engines, Eric asks Erica what the plan is after they pass between the moon and cruise liner. She responds that she is still working on that as hypertravel within the solar system is tricky.

Canta Cee and Albie Thayer return to the bridge. Canta informs George she instructed Albie to turn on all the systems and suggests Phair and Ion do likewise. She asks Dar to be ready with coordinates where the earth and moon are in a straight line and to forward that to Richard, who she asks to plot a course perpendicular to that line.

Dar Skinner jokingly remarks, "The blind leading the blind, Canta?"

But Fashun counters that she thinks she knows where Canta is going and requests to Richard to be ready with the course. Fashun instructs Ion to punch it on her command. George Lee, impressed by the actions his adolescent crew is taking, does not belay their orders.

General Westbrook instructs Erica, George Lee, and Benaiah Body to try their best to stay away from earth's tracking systems as he does not want anyone to suspect the cruise liner is still out there, especially William Kennedy.

"Another lie, General Westbrook?" insinuates the communications engineer.

"You are really starting to irritate me, son," cautions General Westbrook.

J. F. Jones prepares to take his family to Ann Arbor until the violence subsides and to check on the Plummers.

"Oh, the woman whose husband was killed?" ask his wife.

"The news is lying about many things," says JF, "and that is just one of them."

Once in the car, his daughter hears a strange noise and thinks it is coming from the trunk of the car. JF discovers it is coming from David Veil's briefcase, which, along with the other luggage, is still in his vehicle. He tells his family he will drop it off at RNR Industries after he visits the Plummers.

Sharon Plummer awakes from a short nap, hearing her husband, Carl, praying aloud and giving God thanks for sparing his life and that of his lovely wife. His prayer is interrupted when his doctors enter the room, amazed at his rapid recovery, to which he attributes to the grace and mercy of a healing god. They check on him and warn him to get some rest. A nurse enters the room as the doctors are leaving and verifies Carl's need for rest. She is going to allow just one more visitor in the person of J. F. Jones.

Seeing Carl doing so well, J. F. Jones is convinced he wants to be part of whatever religion he and Sharon belong to. J. F. Jones admits he cannot stay as his wife and daughter are in the visitors' lobby and not permitted to visit due to a two-person limit. Sharon politely asks J. F. Jones if he wouldn't mind dropping her off at her home. She wants to get cleaned up a bit before returning back to her husband's side. She also wants someone of his stature to check her home and possibly spend some time with her so she is not alone. The chauffeur is grateful for the opportunity but entreats her that they stop by RNR Industries first to which she has no problem.

Having assembled the staff of RNR Industries in the main conference room, General Westbrook first thanks everyone for their patience and hard work during this crisis. Before he can continue, a security officer escorting a well-dressed gentleman presents the gentleman to Professor Mueller. Everyone in attendance notices what is taking place as well as Elizabeth Devereaux, who walks toward Professor Mueller.

"May I help you?" asks Professor Mueller.

Before the man can answer, Elizabeth Devereaux answers for him. "This is Judge Wright from Detroit. I met with him last Friday to get the hearing moved for Benaiah Boyd. His son is one of the honor students aboard the cruise liner."

Professor Mueller extends his hand toward Judge Wright, who shakes his hand as well as introduces himself to those surrounding him. Judge Wright tells them he wanted to be around when they found out what happened to his son and did not want to hear it on the evening news. General Westbrook welcomes Judge Wright, informing him he is just about to give the staff an update and he is free to join them.

The staff becomes even more attentive to what General Westbrook is about to say in light of Judge Wright's sudden arrival on-site. He then informs them that Eric Miller has made contact with the communications engineer and that Dr. Erica Myers is safely with him. They are currently on board the *Argo Navis*, having left the asteroid Ceres. Most are now bracing for the anticipated bad news that normally follows the good. But General Westbrook is unable to keep a straight face and informs them George Lee and the remaining students have survived the apparent yet unexplained explosion and that their bravery and skills have been of tremendous help to George. There is an immediate eruption of cheers and applause that General Westbrook allows to continue, knowing this crowd needs something to cheer about. One voice in the crowd shouts out and asks General Westbrook to explain what he meant by "remaining students" as the majority of them are unaware that several dozen students were evacuated from the cruise liner and currently in the RNR Industries campus. Having now revealed this, he stresses this information is not common knowledge and not to be publicized to anyone outside this team.

Elizabeth Devereaux asks if anyone knows the status of Benaiah Boyd for which General Westbrook likewise confirms his safety. Knowing Benaiah Boyd is safe causes Elizabeth Devereaux to release a shout thanking Jesus that was subtle yet loud enough for those around her to hear and also praise God.

General Westbrook warns them, however, that the cruise liner is still not out of danger and currently on a crash course with the moon. However, Dr. Myers, David Veil, and Bill Rogers have a plan. He finishes by notifying all the staff to begin preparations for the arrival of all three vessels under the cover of darkness.

7. The Righteous Meet

J. F. Jones, his wife, his daughter, and Sharon Plummer arrive at the main gate of RNR Industries. After business hours, the main entrance gate is no longer manned by a security guard; therefore, J. F. Jones has to use a button on the intercom to request access to the premises. A solid minute passes, and the chauffeur's wife suggests they abandon this trip; however, J. F. Jones persists and waits patiently for an answer. He presses the button again, and within seconds, a man's voice welcomes him to RNR Industries and asks him to state the purpose of his visit. J. F. Jones states his name and explains he is looking for David Veil and Bill Rogers, who he dropped off several hours earlier. He expounds further that they left their baggage in the trunk of his car. The person on the other end of the intercom asks him to wait while he validates his statement. A minute later, the security gate lifts and the person on the other end of the intercom directs him to the main office building. J. F. Jones proceeds as directed and parks his vehicle. While he and his passengers are exiting the limousine, they are approached by a woman extending her hand. J. F. Jones retrieves the briefcase emitting the sound of an incoming phone message from the trunk of his car, deciding to leave the other luggage there for the time being.

"Welcome to RNR Industries, Mr. Jones. I'm Grace Gryer," she says. "Please come with me as we have quite a bit of work going on tonight. David Veil and Bill Rogers indicated you are acquainted with Benaiah Boyd and thought you might want to be here upon his arrival."

They enter the main office building and proceed toward the main conference room.

"Thanks so much for having me, Grace," replies J. F. Jones. "I hope my being here does not create a problem."

"Nonsense, Mr. Jones," replies Grace, opening the door to the main conference room and extending her hand for the quartet of visitors to enter.

J. F. Jones's daughter becomes completely intrigued by the sophisticated audio and video equipment in this highly technical mega meeting room. Noticing her interest, a woman walks over to greet her.

"Hello, my name is Elizabeth Devereaux," says the young woman. "If your parents won't mind, I'd like to show you around. A friend of mine, Benaiah Boyd, is an astronaut who we are expecting to return this evening from outer space."

"Elizabeth Devereaux?" asks Sharon Plummer. "You are Elizabeth Devereaux?"

"Yes, ma'am, I am," answers Elizabeth.

"My name is Sharon Plummer. I believe you are the reason my husband and I returned to Michigan. You are the young woman interested in buying our home. God is truly the ultimate choreographer. Please continue with your young friend. I will touch base with you later, for God has rightly brought me to this place."

Giving her mother a huge hug before walking away, J. F. Jones's excited daughter, while looking back at her father, explains to Elizabeth that Benaiah Boyd and her father are friends. This scenario has a calming effect on J. F. Jones's wife. Seconds later, David Veil and Bill Rogers approach the limo driver. They welcome him and his wife to RNR Industries and thank him for returning the briefcase. J. F. Jones informs David Veil that someone has been attempting to reach him, which is the main reason for their stopping by this facility. J. F. Jones introduces his wife and Sharon Plummer to them. Both men inquire as to how Sharon's husband is doing for which she simply replies that God is great and to be praised.

Sharon Plummer notices a break room adjacent to the large conference room and, taking J. F. Jones's wife by the hand, suggests they go and get some coffee. J. F. Jones's wife, after responding that she would be delighted, parts company with her husband. David Veil and Bill Rogers demand to J. F. Jones to make himself at home and likewise depart his company.

Enabling the forward viewer and opening the sun shield of the *Argo Navis*, Erica Myers insists to Eric Miller to explain why they decided to build totally black spacecraft. She explains she cannot see anything. The moon is within visual range, and while this maneuver alone is dangerous enough, they will also be unable to see the cruise liner before it is too late. The ship is totally under the control of the computers.

On the cruise liner, George has given total command of the vessel to its young crew. Fashun wants Dar Skinner to feed his straight-line coordinates to Richard Wright's navigational console. She instructs Ion Stein to engage the engines with all the power Canta Cee has provided upon her command. Fashun receives the verification that the *Argo Navis* has synchronized the positioning systems of both vessels and they are on a ten-second countdown to execution.

Eric Miller informs the RNR Industries staff, who changes the video monitor to a tracking screen and pipes the graphic presentation to the conference room. All three vessels are now showing up with current-trajectory images on the monitors in the conference room and in the adjacent main control room. All is quiet as everyone on earth, as well as on the three spacecraft, listens to the countdown relative to the positions of the ships' flight paths. Because of the black color of the spacecrafts against the darkness of space and the dark side of the moon, yellow dots indicate the vessels displayed on the screen at RNR Industries.

Erica Myers asks her pilot, Eric Miller, to give her full power as she will need it to execute their course and escape velocity after passing by the cruise liner. Erica has uploaded their escape course to rendezvous with the *Argo Two*. Both the *Argo Navis* and *Argo Two* will slingshot around the sun before executing a warp-to-sudden-stop maneuver to within a hundred miles above RNR Industries. The two spaceships will literally appear as one vessel to RNR Industries' monitors. The trip to the sun will give the cruise liner time and space to make its necessary corrections. All of this is planned to be viewable on RNR Industries' video monitor of the solar system as lightning traveling through space.

Sharon Plummer and J. F. Jones's wife exit the break room to witness this spectacular event. Sharon says a soft prayer and takes hold of the limo driver's wife's hand. A man standing on the opposite side of Sharon Plummer and hearing her prayer takes hold of her free hand. He identifies himself as Judge Wright, thanking her for praying for his son's safe return.

Most of the employees at RNR Industries rush outdoors as the sudden stops of spacecrafts from warp are spectacles to behold. Grace Gryer motions for Sharon Plummer, Judge Wright, and J. F. Jones's wife to follow her outdoors. Once there, they are united with Elizabeth Devereaux and J. F. Jones's daughter. Bill Rogers points to a position in the sky where light trails produced by the *Argo Navis* and *Argo Two* vessels moving at hyperspeed should appear. The ground crews, having been inactive for the past few days, race into action, preparing for the arrival of all three spacecraft. The doors on three aircraft hangars open, and runway lights illuminate. The Argo ships will be stored in hangars at the far end of the facility, and the cruise liner will occupy a hangar adjacent to the control tower.

In the same second the countdown from Erica reaches zero, Dar Skinner, on the bridge of the cruise liner, shouts to Fashun Maddle that he has fed the straight-line coordinates to Richard Wright's navigation console. Validating the coordinates are received and plugging them into his program, Richard shouts to Fashun they are ready to go.

Seconds later, Canta's voice from engineering states that full power has been restored to engineering. Anticipating the success of this maneuver, Erica Myers embedded a subroutine to have the cruise liner follow the same course back to earth upon initiating its hyperdrive engines. To the surprise of the crew on the cruise liner, once Canta's announcement was made, the ship jumps into hyperspace. Fashun inquires as to who executed a hyperjump command to which she receives no immediate answer. After several minutes of silence, Richard Wright informs the bridge crew that Dr. Erica Myers uploaded a program that activated the maneuvers of all three ships once the hyperspace engines on the cruise liner came online. Before he can continue his summary, the ship-to-ship-communications channel opens, and Dr. Myers voice comes across the speakers.

"Welcome back, Cruise Liner. Well done!" she says. "If you open your forward viewer, you will see all three ships are in a low earth orbit and are ready to descend. The control tower at RNR Industries will be awaiting our return, so we should hurry before any earth tracking systems pick us up. See you all on the ground. *Agro Navis* out!"

"Thank you, everyone," insists George Lee. "I'm sure I speak for everyone in this program when I say you have definitely exceeded our expectations. I'm so proud to have been your comrade on this—your first mission. Ion Stein, please move us away from the Argo vessels and prepare for landing."

Ion Stein cracks his knuckles before pressing a single button and affirming, "Engaged, sir. I always wanted to say that."

The reenergized staff at RNR Industries is held back by the ground crews as the huge cruise liner breaks the night sky and hovers over the tarmac. The ground crews drive out a portable landing pad, which will also act as an exit ramp. Further down the runway, the *Argo Navis* and *Argo Two* have arrived, but the black color of the vessels make them hard to make out in the night sky. Because Eric Miller and Benaiah Boyd have been in in the outer regions of the solar system, their vessels will be moved into their respective hangars and placed under an eight-hour quarantine. Unfortunately, Dr. Myers will also have to experience the decontamination process with Eric Miller. Because the teenagers were not in space for an extended period of time, Professor Mueller does not feel it is necessary for the students to go through a decontamination process.

On board the cruise liner, Fashun asks her young crew to report on their perspective systems before exiting the vehicle. Ion Stein tells her that the ship has come to a halt. Phair Ghirl reports that ground crews have contacted them and are ready for them to disembark. Dar Skinner and Richard Wright report that the navigation systems have been taken off-line. Canta Cee interjects that the engines have shut down. Phair Ghirl contacts the ground crews before locking out the pilots' stations. The ground crews' foreman ascends up the ramp and connects the ramp to the area where the crew will exit. Ion Stein gets permission from Fashun Maddle to open the door. Seconds later, the outer ship door slowly opens to a steady stream of applause. The first to exit the ship is Albie Thayer with Canta Cee firmly holding his arm. Next are Ion Stein and Phair Ghirl, followed by Richard Wright and Dar Skinner. Last but not least are George Lee and Fashun Maddle. The applause continues until the last person's feet are on the ground. George Lee signals for one of the night security guards to return to the ship and remove the young man in isolation due to his conduct that nearly cost Dr. Myers her life. He did not want this student to be congratulated with the brave and heroic bridge crew.

Upon seeing his son, Judge Wright clasps his hands together in a prayerlike fashion and lowers his head. His son does not yet realize his father is among those present. Judge Wright weaves his way through the crowd and approaches his son, who looks upon him in surprise. While telling his son only that he loves him, they tightly embrace each other. Judge Wright asks General Westbrook if he may have a few moments alone with his son. General Westbrook grants the request and directs him to a small meeting room inside the hangar where ground crews have started to move the cruise liner.

Everyone present follows behind the cruise liner into the hangar. General Westbrook asks Professor Mueller to follow him to a public-address system. The high-pitched squeal resulting from the system's activation grabs everyone's attention. "May I have your attention, please?" beckons General Westbrook. "I realize it is getting late, but I need all the students to follow Professor Mueller to the campus commons where you will stay the remainder of the night with the other students from your vessel. No one—and I mean no one—is permitted to contact anyone outside this facility. Your parents have been contacted and invited to attend a memorial service for you tomorrow. They are unaware you survived what is being broadcast as the explosion of your ship. You will be reunited with them at that time. We invite all our guests to stay with us as we work on analyzing the events of these past few days. We need to expose those who seek to discredit us and destroy our lives and our organizations. Again, welcome home, young people."

David Veil approaches General Westbrook, informing him that the communications engineer has finished extracting all the data from the drives Bill Rodgers brought with him and will be transferring the audio and video files from the engineering lab to the system in the main conference room. He will be ready to go in about an hour.

On board the *Argo Navis*, Eric Miller and Erica Myers have an opportunity to face each other without any external interruptions or influences. Eric, without saying a word, takes Erica by the hand, escorting her to the ship's lounge. He takes a seat next to her while still holding her hand for which she has made no attempt to loosen from. He starts off by thanking God for allowing them this time of solitude together. But before he can continue, she takes her free hand and puts it on his lips. She then rests her head on his shoulders, shuts her eyes, and falls asleep. He puts his arms around her and does the same.

Sharon Plummer thanks J. F. Jones for bringing her to such a joyous occasion but believes it is time she returned home. She expresses a desire to assist but does not know what she could offer. She does request that he and his family stay with her the night as she does not want to be left alone. They find Elizabeth Devereaux and J. F. Jones's daughter, whom Sharon wants desperately to join them as she realizes Elizabeth is most likely going to be the next owner of her house and figures she might as well get the grand tour. They all agree and are beginning to depart the campus when they are confronted by David Veil. David thanks J. F. Jones for returning his briefcase and phone and will walk to JF's car to retrieve his remaining belongings. David Veil, while walking to the limo, asks J. F. Jones if he wouldn't mind returning to the facility tomorrow when Benaiah Boyd exits the *Argo Two*. He thinks it will be a good idea for Benaiah to see his former lieutenant and learn of his heroics. The two men shake hands and part each other's company.

J. F. Jones makes a quick stop at a grocery store before returning to Sharon Plummer's home. Even while weary from the events of the day and having no time to stock her refrigerator and cupboards, Sharon gives everyone a tour of her residence and suggests to Elizabeth Devereaux to become familiar with her future abode by cooking up something for herself and her guests while she retires to a guest room to call her husband and wish him a good night. J. F. Jones's wife and daughter clean up the master bedroom, tossing the bloody sheets that represent the only signs of the home invasion. Sharon returns to the kitchen where her guests are enjoying themselves to bid them a blessed evening as she will be retiring for the night. The spacious dwelling has more than enough rooms for them to stay, and she asks them to wake her in the morning. They have a television on, but none of them seem to be aware of the broadcast. As Sharon turns to leave the kitchen, the news reporter appears to be interviewing a law-enforcement officer, but no one else is paying any attention. Listening closely, Sharon perceives the police are asking the public to identify a man whose sketched portrait is displayed on the screen.

"That face looks familiar," she mumbles, grabbing the attention of her guests, who look toward the television then back at Sharon. However, the story has ended, and the sketch is gone. Forcing everyone to quiet down, Elizabeth asks Sharon to repeat what she said only to have Sharon reply that she just thought she might have recognized the man on the newscast but attributed it to fatigue. Elizabeth thinks it's strange that Sharon would recognize a man in Michigan, seeing she has been living in Houston. So after politely requesting J. F. Jones's daughter to turn off the television, she inquires further of Sharon where she believes she recognized the man from. The mentioning of Houston triggers Sharon's memory from the airport. She is certain the man was on their flight from Houston. She wanted to tell her husband something about the man but did not get around to it, and now she can't seem to remember.

J. F. Jones enters the conversation, stating they need to contact the Detroit police and let them know the victim might have ties to Houston and maybe they can send his profile to the authorities in Texas to help them solve this mystery.

General Westbrook, Professor Mueller, Bill Rogers, and David Veil examine the video recordings of the Alpha Station taken from the backup files at the Space Agency and determine the video shown to the public has been altered and is not authentic. They strongly believe that the NIA director with revenge as a motive is behind the scheme to discredit the Space Agency, RNR Industries, and its employees and this is the first evidence supporting that theory.

David Veil's satellite phone chimes, indicating an incoming call. He recognizes the caller ID as being his home phone and realizes he has not checked in with his wife since arriving in Michigan. He excuses himself and, while walking a few yards away, answers the call. For the most part, he listens as his wife criticizes him for not checking in. After a few minutes of silence, his three colleagues hear him tell his wife he will give Detective Purkins a call before ending the conversation with these three little words with eight little letters: "I love you." Walking toward his comrades, he checks his voice messages. General Westbrook, Professor Mueller, and Bill Rogers watch as David Veil's facial expression indicates bad news.

"What's going on, David?" asks Bill Rogers.

"I just played back a message from Detective Purkins," he said. "The autopsy results on Helen Hayes reveal she was murdered."

Silence overtakes all four men as they wonder within themselves why someone would kill Helen Hayes. Then Professor Mueller, the only one of the four who did not know Helen all that well, starts to walk away. When asked by General Westbrook if everything was all right, Professor Mueller simply states he is going to his office to work on a theory and wishes them a good night.

In the early morning hours after the eight-hour quarantine expired, a crowd gathers outside the hangars housing the *Argo Navis* and *Argo Two* spacecrafts. Also in attendance are J. F. Jones and his family, Elizabeth Devereaux, and Sharon Plummer. Heads start to turn away from the spaceships as Will Davies approaches the multitude while pushing his wife, Sarah, in a wheelchair. A path is made for them as they head straight to the *Argo Two* hangar. The ground crews open the bay doors to both adjacent hangars, move antigravity platforms into position, and activate the platforms' stair lights. Those who know Eric Miller have not seen him in over a year, while others present have never met him. Bill Rodgers approaches and stands next to J. F. Jones and Elizabeth Devereaux, anxiously waiting for Benaiah Boyd to exit the *Argo Two*.

J. F. Jones asks, "Is it just me, or does everyone else seems more excited about the return of these two Argo ships than they were about the cruise liner with the kids on it?"

Bill Rogers informs him that Eric Miller had been in space for over a year and is a very well respected member of RNR Industries, not to mention his affection toward Dr. Erica Myers. He jokingly adds that rumor has it that Eric Miller and Dr. Myers might not be leaving the ship for which J. F. Jones replies he will be leaving that thought alone.

The *Argo Navis* is the first of the two ships to release its crew. Technologies developed by RNR Industries engineers have made it possible for their ships to activate a built-in decontamination mode while the crews do not leave the vessels. A voice comes across the hangar's intercom system, stating that the decontamination process has ended and it is now safe to open the hatch. After several seconds that seem like an eternity, Eric Miller emerges from the spacecraft and halts at the top of the ramp. The crowd erupts with loud cheers, clapping of hands, and whistles. Right behind him is Dr. Erica Myers. And even if it should not have been possible, the chants and applauds become even louder. The two astronauts wave to the awaiting audience before Eric Miller extends his elbow toward Erica Myers who, after taking him by the arm, proceeds to slowly and deliberately stroll down the ramp. Once at the bottom, they are inundated by all those present. The ceremony continues for several minutes before all attention sways to the adjacent hangar; the *Argo Two* is just moments away from releasing its lone crewman.

As soon as the announcer verifies it is safe to open the hatch, the door opens, revealing a waiting Benaiah Boyd at the top of the ramp. Without hesitation, he starts down the ramp. Halfway down the ramp, Benaiah Boyd sees a man standing next to a woman in a wheelchair and waiting for him. He slows his pace, recognizing them as Will and Sarah Davies. Only Professor Mueller, General Westbrook, Bill Rogers, and David Veil, along with Eric Miller, know the true significance of this encounter, yet no one comes within ten yards of them.

There is silence in the hangar as the once-jubilant crowd wait in anticipation on what will happen next. Benaiah Boyd, as big and tough as he is, starts to weep as he approaches the bottom of the ramp and the Davieses. Will assists his wife, Sarah, to her feet.

"Thank you for saving my life, sir," she says with tears rolling down her face. Releasing her husband, she wraps both her arms around Benaiah Boyd, squeezing him with all her might.

"You are the strongest and bravest woman I know," replies Benaiah Boyd.

William Davies steps beside them and offers his gratitude. "I want to thank you, big brother, for helping us. We would not have made it without you." He too joins his wife in embracing their rescuer.

After a moment of silence and not a dry eye in the place, others start to make their way to Benaiah Boyd's side.

Next in line is Elizabeth Devereaux, who gives Benaiah Boyd a kiss on his lips and, in like fashion as Sarah Davies, squeezes him tight. To Benaiah Boyd's surprise, standing next to Elizabeth Devereaux is J. F. Jones, who shakes the hand of his long-time friend.

"What the heck are you doing here, JF?" asks Benaiah Boyd.

"It's a long story, Boss," states J. F. Jones.

General Westbrook engages the public-address system and announces that he wants all senior staff members and guests to meet immediately in the main conference room. The parents of the students will be arriving in a couple of hours, and Professor Mueller wants to prep everyone prior to their arrival. Bill Rogers tells J. F. Jones he should definitely attend the meeting and be ready to present anything he and Sharon Plummer might have to share. General Westbrook spots Judge Wright in the audience and asks him to please join the staff members as well.

Inside the conference room, General Westbrook once again welcomes the crews of the *Argo Navis*, the *Argo Two*, and the cruise liner, as well as guests new to RNR Industries, back to the planet. He explains they only have a few hours before the parents of the children will arrive for what they were told would be a memorial service for their loved ones, but as everyone there knows, the students are alive and well and will at that time be reunited with their parents. Because General Westbrook expects the news media will be in attendance, he did not want to leak out the true intent of this gathering, and that is to catch the NIA director by surprise, forcing him to admit his guilt and clear their organization. With that said, General Westbrook turns the meeting over to Professor Mueller.

"Good morning, everyone, and thanks for taking the time to meet with us," expresses Professor Mueller. "I've spent most of the night working on this presentation and wanted to share some of it with you so that you will not be surprised when the exhibitions are displayed or when I ask you to give a testimony. Most, if not all, of what you have heard from the media is incorrect and a lie. We have evidence supporting everything that we know to be true, whether it concerns the Alpha Station, the cruise liner, or the thugs posing as gang members terrorizing our community—who are in no way affiliated with the citizens we have partnered with formally known as B-Square. A friend loyal to General Westbrook is holding an exclusive story that his network will not release until after our memorial service. We are expecting and earnestly anticipating both local and national news networks to be in attendance. I am confident the villain we all believe is behind this will be exposed and brought to justice for his crimes against our organization.

"In the hangar of the cruise liner, we have a stage set up a few yards in front of the vessel. With the public expecting the ship was destroyed, they will be curious but will not think twice about seeing another such ship. The students are entering the vessel as we speak. We have over two hundred chairs for our guests, facing the podium. On the stage will be myself, General Westbrook, David Veil, and Bill Rogers. However, there will be a dozen or so empty chairs for the righteous individuals for which our enemies have wrongfully accused and who have sacrificed their time. Once they have been vindicated, they will remain on the podium. Above and behind these chairs is a large cinema screen where certain video clips will be replayed."

All heads turn around as two gentlemen walk into the conference room, escorted by Grace Gryer. Professor Mueller asks them to come forth and for David Veil to introduce them.

"Thank you, Professor Mueller," acknowledges David Veil. Stretching out his arm toward the first man, he introduces him to everyone gathered. "This is Detective Purkins from Houston and his partner, Detective Majours. They have some information they want to share concerning the death of Helen Hayes. They arrived early this morning and have spent some time with the Detroit police as well as the friend of General Westbrook. They are going to share with us some disturbing findings that we trust will help bring this all together. I believe Sharon Plummer is in attendance, is she not? The detectives would like to speak to you for a few moments after we dismiss."

A surprised Sharon stands and introduces herself to the detectives. General Westbrook dismisses the staff and friends and asks them to stay in the conference room until called upon.

8. Destruction of Disbelief

As parents of students arrive at RNR Industries for the memorial service, the first things they notice are the massive size of the campus and its resemblance to an airport. The office buildings and manufacturing plants are similar to airport terminals at first glance. Also arriving are tens of local and national news crews. Security guards direct all the guests to parking attendants standing on the tarmac in front of a huge hangar. As the guests enter the hangar, refreshments are provided, but the atmosphere is quiet and somber. The only noise emanating from the hangar is that of the camera crews setting up their equipment. Some ponder in their hearts why they have to meet in a hangar in front of a huge ship that they imagine to be another cruise liner, but grief has suppressed any felt ill emotions toward this organization. Hundreds of thousands of households have tuned in to the telecast, including NIA director William Kennedy, who is sitting at his Washington, DC, office desk.

No different from any other well-organized event, Professor Mueller approaches the podium microphone at exactly the top of the hour. He taps the microphone and then speaks the word *testing* several times as the communications engineer adjusts the sound levels. "Welcome, everyone, to the campus of RNR

Industries," he says. "We are extremely honored to have you in our midst. My name is Professor Mueller, CEO and director here at RNR Industries." Pointing to behind himself on the podium, he introduces David Veil and Bill Rogers from the Space Agency in Houston. He then introduces General Westbrook and invites him to the microphone.

General Westbrook thanks all those in attendance who have come out to honor the students. He likewise thanks the news crews for coming out to broadcast this event to the nation and the world. He continues, focusing his eyes in the direction of the news media, and states that the Space Agency and its affiliate, RNR Industries, have come under criticism and been accused of several disturbing acts for which he desired to address before honoring the parents and students of the cruise liner.

"In order to fully understand what happened to the cruise liner," General Westbrook explains, "we need to first take a look at an event that we believe put these children in harm's way. As most of you in the audience and the general public are aware, it was reported several days ago that a planned test flight of an RNR Industries spacecraft identified as the *Argo Two* was involved in an incident with a deep-space outpost called the Alpha Station, which happened to be operated through a joint collaboration with RNR Industries and the Space Agency under my command. The *Argo Two*'s inaugural test flight and first solo flight of its pilot, Mr. Benaiah Boyd, included passing by the civilian-occupied deep-space facility. This facility employed two married scientists: William Davies and his wife, Sarah. These young scientists were on a mission to determine if the region of space just kilometers away could be attributed with having regenerative powers. While it should not matter, Mr. Boyd was the former leader of a Detroit street gang known as B-Square. It was reported that Mr. Boyd was killed when he, for no apparent reason, destroyed the space station, ending his life and the lives of the custodians, William and Sarah Davies. I would like to refute that allegation with proof of what really took place that day. But first, let me introduce to you, alive and well, Mr. Benaiah Boyd."

Benaiah Boyd walks to the podium, escorted by Elizabeth Devereaux. The parents of the students are visibly disturbed by the presence of Benaiah Boyd but sit patiently, expecting this will all result in a logical explanation of the deaths of their children. The two embrace General Westbrook, and all three take their seats as the lights in the hangar dim. David Veil steps to the microphone. Pointing to the screen behind him, he warns those in the audience as well as the television viewers that what they are about to see might be disturbing. NIA director William Kennedy pushes his chair back, rises from behind his desk, and stands in front of his television.

"What I am about to show you are two versions of the incident at the Alpha Station. The first is the video that NORAD, under the direction of the NIA, provided the networks, and the second is what I have been able to salvage from backup-computer files at the Space Agency. I would like to give a special thanks to my colleague Bill Rodgers and the communications engineer here at RNR Industries."

He invites everyone's attention to the video-monitoring screen. The image is very clearly the *Argo Two* spaceship docking to the Alpha Station. Minutes later, the ship leaves at hyperspeed, and the station explodes. David Veil once again reminds everyone this video was shown around the world. David Veil asks the communications engineer to replay the video feed a frame at a time and points to places where the images were spliced using sophisticated, state-of-the-art equipment. He reiterates how impossible it would be to have this much detail from actual footage retrieved millions of miles away. David Veil also highlights other areas where the ship is moving but the stars are not. He points to a blank spot on the video that would normally indicate the time stamp. David Veil signals for the communications engineer to start the video recording taken from the Alpha Station's external cameras, which were constantly sending images back to the Space Agency. At normal speed, the video clearly shows a drone launched from the station that, for no apparent reason, abruptly veers off course. Rewinding the tape and running it at a frame every second, he shows that the absence of stars forms the outline of an object similar to the size of the *Argo Two*. This black outline moves directly in the path of the drone, causing the drone to strike it with enough force to damage it and alter its trajectory. David Veil suggests that whatever technology was used to mask the ship from electronic sensors cannot insert stars in its place. The communications engineer splits the screen with the left side displaying footage from inside the Alpha Station's control room, where the Davieses were working, and the right side displaying footage from the cargo bay. An armed soldier dressed in battle fatigues appears out of nowhere, entering the station through the cargo bay. Because the Space Agency wanted to honor the privacy of the Davieses, video records were made throughout the station with the exception of their living quarters. No audio was recorded—again with the intention of honoring the Davieses' privacy. The armed soldier is seen on several cameras, marching directly toward the control room. Just before the soldier enters the control room, the right side of the monitor shows the *Argo Two* entering the cargo bay. Seconds later, Benaiah Boyd is seen exiting his spacecraft, taking a few steps, and then falling straight back as if he walked right into an invisible wall. David Veil is convinced this is the soldier's cloaked ship. On the left side of the monitor, the soldier enters the control room, and the Davieses appear to welcome him. The soldier apparently asks them a question to which they obviously refuse, resulting in him striking William Davies in the stomach with his weapon. Benaiah Boyd enters the control room, surprising the gunman. Sarah rushes to assist her husband, and the soldier shoots her. Benaiah Boyd darts quickly behind the soldier, reaching across the shooter's shoulders, and grabs both sides of the soldier's rifle, pulling the weapon toward the soldier's neck. The soldier discharges several rounds from his rifle before Benaiah Boyd sticks his right knee into the soldier's back and, with his strength, continues to pull the soldier backward before allowing him to fall on his back. Benaiah Boyd takes possession of the soldier's weapon and makes like he is going to strike the soldier in the face with the butt of the rifle but instead runs to the rescue of Sarah Davies. Applying pressure to her wound and noticing one of her shoes has come off, he removes her sock and places it on her wound to stop the bleeding. Neither Benaiah Boyd nor a frantic William Davies notices the soldier as he escapes the room and vanishes out of sight in the cargo bay. Benaiah Boyd appears to be comforting a hysterical William Davies as he carries Sarah Davies to the *Argo Two*. Seconds later, the *Argo Two* exits the Alpha Station like a bolt of lightning. The communications engineer collapses the video back into a single view and fast forwards the tape to the end where several hours elapse with the station still intact.

The lights in the hangar return to full strength. David Veil returns to his seat, and General Westbrook returns to the podium. Calling the audience's attention again to his right, General

Westbrook announces, "Now here to validate what we have seen on this video, please welcome home, alive and well, William and Sarah Davies."

Pushing his wife in a wheelchair to the side of the stage, William reaches for Sarah's hand as she indicates her desire to walk up the stairs onto the stage. Those on the podium stand and cheer, invoking the same salutation from the audience and news crews. Sarah and William shake General Westbrook's hand while remaining at the podium. A small gathering of reporters storm the stage, but General Westbrook indicates he will entertain questions at the end of this presentation.

After a moment of silence, William Davies speaks out, "Hello. My name is William Davies, but my friends call me Will. My wife, Sarah, and I are or, shall I say, were scientists on the Alpha Station. Our primary assignment was to monitor the activity in the region of space where the spaceship *Argo Navis* created a tear in space as it flew at hyperspeed toward the constellation Cygnus. Drones were sent out at the exact speed and coordinates of the *Argo Navis* in attempts to reproduce the tear. One of these drones unexpectedly and for no apparent reason veered off course. Not being able to determine what caused this phenomenon, we looked for a solution. We were informed by the Space Agency that a ship would be in the area but had no plans of making contact with us."

William Davies's voice starts to crackle; he begins to tremble, and his wife, Sarah, still standing at his side, begins to cry. Will asks if she wants him to stop, but she insists he continue.

"Not able to determine what made the drone veer off course, we decided to contact the *Argo Two* and have the pilot take a look as his ship passed by the station. About an hour later, our internal motion sensors detected movement in the outer cargo bay, where the drones are stored. We assumed it was Benaiah Boyd, the pilot of the *Argo Two*, but wondered why he did not signal us of his arrival and intention to come on board the station. Seconds later, a soldier broke into the main door of our control room and pointed a high-caliber weapon at us. He demanded access to the video-monitoring system. When I refused, he hit me in the stomach with his gun, breaking several ribs. When Sarah came to my rescue, the butthead shot her."

With tears running down his face, Will Davies is unable to continue and becomes weak in his legs. Benaiah Boyd hurries to Will and Sarah Davies and assists them to their seats. Will Davies wipes the tears away from his eyes and suggests to Benaiah Boyd to finish the account of the incident on the Alpha Station.

Holding the cordless microphone and standing behind the chairs occupied by Will and Sarah Davies and with one arm comforting them, Benaiah Boyd resumes the story from his perspective. "In visible range of the station, my sensors only displayed the Alpha Station and what Will Davies describes as a drone several kilometers away from the station. Circling around the back side of the station, I noticed the bay doors to the station were open but no vessel inside of it. I checked my systems again and was not surprised when nothing registered on my sensors or my visual inspection of the bay. The spirit of the Lord led me to go on board the station and check on the Davieses. As soon as I exited the *Argo Two*, I walked into something. I now believe it was a cloaked ship. I started walking to where I believed the control room to be. Entering the control room, I found a man in army fatigues holding an assault rifle. I believe I surprised him as much as he surprised me. With the soldier having turned to approach me, Sarah took the opportunity to check on her husband. I suspect her sudden motions took the gunman by surprise, and he fired. My street prowess took over, thinking that if he shot an innocent woman, he would have no reservation with shooting me. So I ran up behind him and, reaching over his shoulders, grabbed hold of his weapon. The butthead seemed really weak for a soldier and provided little resistance as I pulled the rifle to his neck, making sure the barrel was not pointing toward the Davieses. Starting to lose consciousness, the weakling clown started falling backward, and I let him hit the floor. I wanted badly to finish him off by knocking him on his head but knew that wasn't the godly thing to do. I figured I had time to tie him up before he regained consciousness, so I introduced myself to Will and Sarah Davies. Sarah was conscious but bleeding badly. As a former gang member, I've seen much-worse injuries but knew we were millions of miles from earth and her chances for survival rested on leaving the station as soon as possible. I assisted the Davieses to the *Argo Two* and figured on leaving the butt-wipe gunman but decided to bring him along for proof of what happened. However, when I looked around, he was gone. One of Sarah's shoes had come off, so I used her sock on her wound. Not knowing what was happening or who to trust, I contacted Eric Miller on the asteroid Ceres and flew as fast as I could to get there. Once we arrived on the asteroid, Sarah was unconscious with her condition worsening. Eric Miller, using an experimental transport room connected to his home on earth, transported Sarah and Will there. Grace Gryer met them there, and until a few minutes ago, I did not know if Sarah survived or not, but I thank God she did." Putting his arms around them and giving them a group hug, Benaiah Boyd concludes, "These two individuals are very brave people." Before handing the microphone to General Westbrook, Benaiah Boyd interjects, "Oh yeah, I do not know what happened to the gunman."

Returning to the podium, General Westbrook lowers his head and addresses the parents. "Now it is time to pay tribute to the brave young people on board the cruise liner. This organization believes the soldier's next plan after destroying the Alpha Station was to take aim and destroy the cruise liner. Because of the actions of seven exceptional students, we have proof that the same vessel that visited the Alpha Station also made its way to the cruise liner."

General Westbrook explains that he will call the name of each student in the alphabetical order of the students' last names and directs the parents to please come to the podium from his left. After the name of the first student is called, his parents come to the podium, and to their surprise, they shout and scream for joy as they witness their child emerging from the cruise liner and approaching the podium from the right to meet his parents. A stunned crowd starts to murmur as the second student's name is called and his parents hasten to the podium to see if they will have the same fortuitous pleasure to be reunited with their child. After that pupil emerges and is united with his parents, all the other parents stand, crying with tears of joy and anticipating their loved ones' names will be read off next and earnestly expecting they will appear. This continues until the second-to-the-last student has been reunited with his or her parents. There are screams and shouts for joy as the crowd of parents is completely taken by surprise at what has just transpired. No more surprised is William Kennedy, laying both his arms on the television monitor and speculating what will happen next. General Westbrook gives the crowd a few moments to embrace their children before politely asking the children to stand off to the side and asking their parents to return to their seats.

The last child to be acknowledged is Richard Wright. Coming out to embrace their son are Judge Wright and his wife. The judge pauses at the podium. Not knowing what to expect, General Westbrook steps aside, giving Judge Wright the microphone and permission to speak.

"Please pardon me, ladies and gentlemen, but for those who do not know me, I am Judge Wright, a district-court judge in the city of Detroit. I thank General Westbrook for allowing me to say a few words and, most of all, for bringing my son Richard home safely. If I may add, prior to the launch of the cruise liner and the *Argo Two*, I was approached by NIA director William Kennedy. The NIA director was in town, attempting to persuade me to move against Mr. Benaiah Boyd, a member of the RNR Industries team. Mr. Boyd's counsel, Ms. Devereaux, can validate my story. And for what it's worth, I am ashamed of my actions and thoughts toward this organization. I have witnessed and, without doubt, believe the men I knew as B-Square gangbangers are indeed rehabilitated and have become productive members of our society. I have a completely renewed faith in organizations like RNR Industries and their relentless endeavors to give these young men opportunities to succeed. Furthermore, I do not believe any of them are linked to the terrorist activities they are reported to have committed. Thank you."

Stepping away from the microphone, Judge Wright shakes General Westbrook's hand and exits the podium together with his wife and son. Richard Wright joins the bridge crew while his parents return to their seats.

General Westbrook requests the seven students who comprised the bridge crew as well as George Lee to join him on the stage. He tells those in the audience as well as those viewing in their homes that the quick thinking and reactions of these young men and women not only saved their own lives and the cruise liner docked behind them but also provided the first clues to the fact that a cloaked ship was in the area. General Westbrook instructs George Lee to hand them certificates as he introduces each person. He first recognizes Fashun Maddle for her leadership skills in taking command of the vessel. Next to be commended are Ion Stein and Phair Ghirl for their piloting skills. Following Ion and Phair are Canta Cee and Albie Thayer, praised for their support in engineering. Finally, he acknowledges Richard Wright and Dar Skinner for their navigational skills.

"These seven students were faced with an unusual task," explains General Westbrook. "On board the cruise liner was an experimental transport room designed by an RNR scientist, Eric Miller—who was, at the time, on a rock in the asteroid belt. The only other senior member of the cruise liner, Dr. Erica Myers, became trapped in this room. This crew needed to jump into hyperspace in order to generate enough energy to free Dr. Myers from the room. However, before making the jump into hyperspace, Richard and Dar transferred their data to David Veil and Bill Rogers. These two talented and exceptional young scientists discovered something off the bow of the ship and refused to chalk it up as a mysterious phenomenon." General Westbrook explains that there was still one important detail that has not yet been explained. "Seeing it is apparent the cruise liner was not destroyed, what caused the explosion?" General Westbrook calls to the podium David Veil and Bill Rogers.

David Veil, a former mission-control director, picks up from where General Westbrook left off and explains that Richard and Dar modified the navigational arrays to sense for temperature variations outside the ship. "These temperature-variation algorithms can be applied to both current data as well as recorded data. These two exceptional young scientists applied their theory to the exterior of the cruise liner and forwarded the results to Bill and me just before jumping into hyperspace." Pointing to the screen behind him, he exposes the image after applying the temperature-variation program. "This, ladies and gentleman, is the outline of a cloaked spaceship. We have compared this design to those in our database and confirm it is of Soviet origin. Furthermore and of equal importance, we were able to track the specific heat signature of this vessel and its trajectory through space. It indeed was the invisible ship that visited the Alpha Station. We also know it was launched from somewhere in the Soviet Republic. We were hoping to have the exact coordinates before today's program. Ironically enough, this specific temperature pattern ended with the explosion previously thought to be the cruise liner. We speculate it was intentionally planned to detonate, destroying the pilot along with the evidence the ship visited the Alpha Station—not to mention planting a seed of doubt regarding the integrity of the collaboration between the Space Agency and RNR Industries."

Once again, members of the news media rush the podium with questions, and as before, General Westbrook refuses to comment until after all the facts have been presented and the truth revealed.

In his Washington, DC, office, NIA director William Kennedy has heard enough and believes it is a matter of time before he is linked to this scandal. Using a flash drive, he begins to remove data from his computer. While files are being downloaded, he quickly retrieves paper files connecting him to a group of Soviet shipbuilders—the same organization that seized schematics from

RNR Industries and built the doomed replica of the *Argo Navis* that killed his brother.

Professor Mueller returns to the podium. "Now that we have recognized the achievements of the living, it is time to pay tribute to those who have suffered and lost their lives in defense of the Space Agency and RNR Industries. Having no knowledge such an elaborate plot existed at the time of her death, we now know our beloved colleague Helen Hayes was the first to lose her life at the hands of wicked men. Ms. Hayes was a healthy and beloved employee of the Space Agency and the executive secretary of General Westbrook. Last week, she was found dead in her car outside her Houston, Texas, home. In the vehicle with her body were video tapes taken from Space Agency computers as well as her security badge. These tapes held the same falsified accounts of the destruction of the space station. Logs taken from the security system revealed her security badge was used to gain entrance into the computer-data center and the video-monitoring systems after her estimated time of death. The news media, without validating the tapes' contents, began their assault on the integrities of the Space Agency and RNR Industries. As proven earlier, these tapes were not genuine. The hospital initially ruled that Helen Hayes died as a result of a heart attack, but the medical examiner's report indicated she had been given a lethal injection of a paclitaxel-mitoxantrone cocktail, having discovered a puncture wound on her neck. This, in itself, was cause enough for detectives to start a murder investigation. It wasn't until later that a neighbor of Ms. Hayes, Sharon Plummer, who is visiting Michigan, recognized a victim from a Detroit homicide as a man seen in the car with Ms. Hayes on the day of her death. He was also seen on the flight from Houston to Detroit and at the airport in Detroit. Houston detectives traveling to Detroit and using forensic evidence were able to connect this man to Helen Hayes's murder. In what first seemed to be an unrelated incident, several men impersonating B-Square gang members started a wave of violent attacks, which began with the murder of this same man in an alley of a Detroit bar. A witness in the bar, using his satellite phone, took a picture of the pair escorting the victim into the alley. These two men were later identified by a limousine driver at a local coffee shop. It just happens that this limousine driver, J. F. Jones, was a former B-Square gang lieutenant and immediately identified them as impostors. He further tracked them to the home of Sharon Plummer, whom he had transported earlier that evening. Police believe the mastermind of this operation was attempting to leave no trace of his involvement in the murder of Helen Hayes. We suspect our nemesis believed the local authorities or, better yet, a legitimate B-Square gang member would eventually apprehend and kill these impostors. Now for that breaking news you have all been seeking. A local law-enforcement agent loyal to General Westbrook and sympathetic to his cause apprehended these juvenile delinquents late last night, turning them over to federal authorities without leaking the story to the press. It appears these thugs were not smart enough to dispose of the phone used to communicate to the man orchestrating these events. This man is none other than NIA director William Kennedy."

NIA director William Kennedy slowly opens his office door leading to the hallway, sticking his head out and checking to make sure the path to the stairway is clear of personnel. Rushing down the stairs to the private underground parking lot in the same manner he left his office, William Kennedy pokes his head out of the stairway doors. Believing the route is clear, he proceeds in a straight line to his car. Just feet away and using his remote starter, he unlocks the doors and starts the engine. However, as he reaches for the door handle to enter his vehicle, he is apprehended by federal agents and arrested.

All those in the audience stand as Professors Mueller summons Eric Miller to the podium to give a closing prayer concluding the services. After it, instead of rushing toward the podium, the news crews scramble to make sure they are the first to air this breaking news and contact their affiliates in Washington. One reporter, certain to gain an exclusive story, approaches the podium. Unaware that the microphone is still on, the reporter asks Professor Mueller and Eric Miller if they could settle once and for all the question of whether or not the Cygnus region of space has any healing properties. Before Eric Miller could give an answer, all those remaining in the hangar turn and focus their full attention toward the podium. Erica Myers joins the duo and takes hold of Eric Miller's arm. Briefly but poignantly Eric Miller explains that Dr. Erica Myers was healed of her crippled leg as a direct result of a God-answered prayer that had nothing to do with this Cygnus region of space. He then prays for the safe return home of the students and their families and dismisses the program.

Proud of what Eric told the reporters and sensing an excellent opportunity to tell him of her adventure in the experimental room on board the cruise liner, Erica asks Eric if there is some place private they could go. Eric suggests they board the *Argo Navis* as no one would suspect to look for them there. Without drawing any attention to themselves, they borrow a two-seated tarmac truck and head toward the *Argo Navis* hangar.

Judge Wright approaches Elizabeth Devereaux and Benaiah Boyd. "Please pardon me, Ms. Devereaux and Mr. Boyd," begs Judge Wright. "I just wanted to apologize for the way I treated you and this case. I want you to know that the events of the past few days have caused me to destroy my disbelief that thugs, for lack of a better word, could genuinely become rehabilitated. Therefore, on tomorrow morning, I am going to dismiss the case and all charges against you with the exception of your failing to appear in court. For that, I will sentence you to thirty days of community service. I would like for you to speak to students in Detroit public schools and other regional school districts and address the advantages of leaving a gang mentality and getting opportunities in education and science."

"Thank you, Judge Wright," replies Benaiah Boyd, extending his hand to shake hands with the judge. "It would be my pleasure and an honor."

J. F. Jones, his family, and Sharon Plummer approach Benaiah Boyd and Elizabeth Devereaux. J. F. Jones explains that Sharon Plummer is going to take him and his family to her church on Packard Road. Benaiah Boyd comments that he was baptized in Jesus's name and filled with God's spirit at the apostolic church that Eric Miller attends. He continues to explain it was there he met Elizabeth. Once he gave them the address and the pastor's name, Sharon confesses that was the same church she attended years ago before moving to Texas and the church they would be heading to. They browse the audience to look for Eric Miller to see if he wanted to join them but did not locate him. They decide to leave without him. On the way to the church, Elizabeth reminds Benaiah that he is going to explain to her how he came about with such an unusual name.

145

"I nearly died during childbirth, according to my God-fearing mother," explains Benaiah. "She prayed to God in the hospital that I would live and be strong. While in the hospital and reading her Bible one day, the spirit of the Lord led her to read about a soldier in King David's army. She said that in the first book of Chronicles, in its eleventh chapter's twenty-second and twenty-third verses, there was a valiant man who slew two lionlike men of Moab, slew a lion in a pit in a snowy day, and slew an Egyptian of great statue who, having a spear in his hand, went down to him, and he plucked the spear out of the Egyptian's hand and slew him with his own spear. She told me that prior to reading this story, she did not believe I would survive the streets of Detroit. But having read about this combatant destroyed her disbelief concerning my future. The warrior's name was Benaiah."

On board the *Argo Navis*, Eric Miller and Erica Myers, using the ship's command console, lock out all functions, guaranteeing their privacy. They find their way to the ship's lounge, the room where Eric encountered Erica sleeping on their maiden voyage with thoughts of putting her to sleep. The two sit next to each other on the couch. Erica starts out by asking Eric to listen to all she has to say without interruptions to which he agrees. For the most part, Eric is excited to hear what she has to say, but there is a bit of apprehension, and he hopes this is not some sort of final good-bye for forever or is not a work speech. Erica begins by taking Eric's hands into hers and expressing that what she is about to tell him is absolutely the truth. She says that when she was locked in the experimental transport room on the cruise liner, it was pitch-black. The only thing she had with her was a language translator given to her by Fashun Maddle. Within minutes of entering the room, she believes she fell asleep and started to dream. In her dream, she discovered she was not alone and that a man also occupied the room or her mind or however he might want to look at it. In his mind, Eric starts to think this is going to be a rape confession but tries to keep an open mind. Erica says the man was speaking an unknown language. It was not until she realized she had the universal language translator that she was able to communicate with the man, who said his name was Philip. She says the man was obviously from a land where technology was not available and actually thought she was an angel and that he was in heaven. Having convinced Philip she was not an angelic being and the room was not heaven, she says they sat down next to each other and started having a conversation about Jesus even though he was not aware of the Bible, which she thought was strange. She says Philip said he was sitting with a black man and talking to him just like he was talking to Erica. She says he told Erica the last thing he remembered before being brought to the room was having baptized this man in a river. Erica says she could not dispute what he was saying because his clothes were wet. Then Erica says Philip asked her a very strange question: He wanted to know what was hindering her from being saved, and she said she did not know what she needed to be saved from except the room.

"So tell me, Eric," pleads Erica, "did you program this room to decrease the oxygen levels so that someone in the room would be rendered unconscious?"

"I would never do that, Erica," admits Eric.

"So what do you think of this dream?" asks Erica. "Do you think I'm crazy?"

"No, I don't think you are crazy, Ricky, and to tell you the truth, my explanation might cause you to believe I am a little nuts," replies Eric. "But before I examine your so-called dream, I need to tell you something."

"By all means, go ahead," begs Erica.

"Regardless of what happens to us after this, I need you to know that I love you and always have ever since that skating party in elementary school," confesses Eric Miller. "Two years ago after our return from Cygnus, I was rather rough on you and insensitive to the pain you felt with the loss of your mother. I am deeply sorry for that and beg your forgiveness."

"I love you too, Eric, and all is forgiven," declares Erica as she thinks within herself she never expected a man to tell her he loved her before she admitted it to him first.

"My prayer," continues Eric, "is that we not only have the occasion to meet like this but that God would also cause something to happen in your life to reveal himself to you. My faith and belief is that I will have a lifelong companion who shares the same spiritual beliefs that I do. When I thought I had pushed you away, I thought there was no way I could do anything to win you back, let alone to Christ."

"Oh, Eric, you don't know how much I respect you for being a godly man. But to tell you the truth, I know little, if anything, about the Bible, and that embarrasses me. But when I was locked in that room and thought I was going to die, you and God were the only things occupying my mind. I don't know how prayer works, but I believed you were praying for me. You have a godly spirit, and I want that too. Now tell me what you think about this dream I had," beseeches Dr. Myers.

"Well," starts Eric as he pulls out his pocket computer, "I don't think you had a dream. Read with me some scriptures out of the King James Version of the Bible and then tell me what you think."

Starting with the book of Acts in its eighth chapter's twenty-sixth verse, Eric asks Erica to start reading. "And the angel of the Lord spake unto Philip, saying, 'Arise and go toward the south unto the way that goeth down from Jerusalem unto Gaza, which is desert.'" Erica pauses and, looking up at Eric, says, "This man is Philip." She continues reading. "And he arose and went, and behold, a man of Ethiopia, an eunuch of great authority under Candace, queen of the Ethiopians, who had the charge of all her treasure and had come to Jerusalem for to worship." Erica pauses once again, looking up at Eric, and says, "So this is the black man the Philip in my dream spoke of."

Suddenly, Erica begins to shiver, telling Eric that she is frightened, but Eric encourages her to continue on.

"Was returning and sitting in his chariot read Esaias the prophet. Then the Spirit said unto Philip, 'Go near and join thyself to this chariot.' And Philip ran thither to him and heard him read the prophet Esaias and said, 'Understandest thou what thou readest?'"

With Erica looking at him since he unintentionally seems as if he is going to tell her to stop, he only nods his head, prompting her to read on.

"And he said, 'How can I except some man should guide me?' And he desired Philip that he would come up and sit with him. The place of the scripture which he read was this: *'He was led as a sheep to the slaughter, and like a lamb dumb before his shearer, so opened he not his mouth.'*" Turning around so that she is face-to-face with Eric, Erica asks, "Might this be Jesus?"

Eric simply responds, "You are very smart, my love, and all your questions are soon to be answered. Keep on reading until the end of the chapter." Eric gets up, walks over to a cabinet, retrieves a blanket, returns, and wraps it around a shivering Erica. Now sitting behind her, he wraps both his arms around her stomach and, pointing to verse thirty-three, nudges Erica to continue.

"*In his humiliation, his judgment was taken away. And who shall declare his generation? For his life is taken from the earth.*' And the eunuch answered Philip and said, 'I pray thee, of whom speaketh the prophet this? Of himself or of some other man?'"

Shaking her head up and down and believing she has answered her own question, Erica continues to read. "Then Philip opened his mouth and began at the same scripture and preached unto him Jesus." Erica smiles and, leaning her head back, gives Eric a kiss on his cheek and whispers, "Jesus." Leaning forward, Erica continues to read and now a little faster. "And as they went on their way, they came unto a certain water, and the eunuch said, 'See here is water. What hinder me to be baptized?' And Philip said, 'If thou believest with all thine heart, thou mayest.' And he answered and said, 'I believe that Jesus Christ is the son of God.' And he commanded the chariot to stand still, and they went down both into the water, both Philip and the eunuch. And he baptized him." Erica stops reading and, leaning her head back on Eric's shoulder, asks him if he would baptize her for she remembered he is a deacon in his church.

"I would love to see you baptized," answers Eric, "but don't you want to finish reading the remaining two verses?" he asks.

Erica Myers, still laying her head softly on Eric's chest, closes her eyes and requests he read the remaining two verses to her. Her thoughts return to the transport room, and she recalls that Philip's clothes were wet and had a funny smell to them. She starts to ponder how a dream could be so vivid and real. The Philip in her dream told her that all the things she had just read had happened to him just prior to his arrival in the room.

Now Eric picks up reading where Erica left off. "And when they were come up out of the water, the spirit of the Lord caught away Philip—that the eunuch saw him no more. And he went on his way, rejoicing. And Philip was found at Azotus, and passing through, he preached in all the cities till he came to Caesarea."

Bearing in mind what Eric had just read, Erica rephrases what Eric had just read. "So the Philip in my dream told me he had just come from baptizing the black man. And you read in the Bible that after baptizing the black man or eunuch, Philip disappeared."

"That's right, my love," agrees Eric. "I believe when Philip left the earth over two thousand years ago after baptizing the Ethiopian, God brought Philip to you to convince you."

But before Eric can continue, Erica starts to shout aloud strange sounds. Eric recognizes this as the spirit of God coming upon Erica by evidence of the speaking in an unfamiliar dialect. Erica continues to speak these unknown tongues for several minutes before stopping.

"*What was that?*" she asks. "What just happened to me?"

Eric explains that God's Holy Spirit had come upon her. Erica responds that she has never felt this much vigor, joy, and life. Dr. Myers insists she wants to be baptized before the day ends, so Eric takes her to his church on Packard. On the way there, he has her read Acts 2. When they arrive, the service is just about over. Eric spots Benaiah Boyd and Elizabeth Devereaux shouting and praising God. An usher escorts Eric Miller and Erica Myers to join them. When the altar call is made, Erica knows exactly what she needs to do. Leaving her seat, she approaches an altar worker who escorts her to a small dressing room. J. F. Jones likewise approaches a male altar worker, requesting to be baptized. Having prepared her for baptism, Eric watches as they bring his friend to the water. Erica notices Eric, but as soon as her feet touch the water, she once again shouts praises to God in an unknown language. Even while she is baptized, she continues to speak fluently.

Eric waits for what seems to be an eternity before his friend Dr. Erica Myers returns from the dressing room. "How do you feel, my love?" he asks.

"I feel like a new person," she responds and passionately embraces him. "I have destroyed all my disbelief in God and in your affection toward me."

The altar worker approaches Eric and Erica and asks him if he and Erica are an item.

"Yes, we are," he replies.